THE DANCER'S DAUGHTER

'They are fighting,' she whispered. 'Isabel —
they are fighting.'
Behind the heavy door Courtney's voice could
be heard shouting, 'I'll kill you — I'll kill you
one day. What I do is my own business and
you have no right to question me.'
There was the sound of a struggle, and then a
cry, and the door flew open and Courtney,
panting, tie loose, a bruise across his bleeding
lips, stood staring at us as though he had
never seen us before. His mother ran to him,
but he thrust her aside and went across the
hall to the main door, plunging out into the
night like a drunken man.

The Dancer's Daughter

Josephine Edgar

CORONET BOOKS
Hodder and Stoughton

First published in Great Britain 1968
William Collins Sons & Co. Ltd.

Coronet Edition 1976

Printed and bound in Great Britain for
Coronet Books, Hodder and Stoughton, London
By Cox & Wyman Ltd, London, Reading and Fakenham

ISBN 0 340 20773 6

CHAPTER ONE

The day when my life was changed out of all recognition I went blackberrying in the fields towards Dane's Dyke. I was thirteen, getting to an age when I should have been helping my aunt in the house, scrubbing the red brick floors and setting the bread to rise. Mrs. Bawtry, or Aunt Bessy, as I called her then, was hard-working, rough and practical. I was a dreamer and, as she often said, was 'neither a help nor a hindrance' to her, which meant I was often in the way, so we were both relieved on that bright, windy Saturday afternoon in September when she told me to take a basket of herring to Mrs. Oldroyd, the coachman's wife over at Sutherdyke Hall, and ask for some apples in return and pick some blackberries for a pie on my way across the fields.

'Tha'll be out of my road, that way,' she said impatiently, smacking the bread dough in the red earthenware crock as though it was my impatient, restless, disconcerted self. 'Tha's no more use in t'ouse than a hen. But it's no more than folk can expect from a dancer's daughter.'

That was all I knew about my parents — that my mother had been a dancer. It was the only fact about my birth that my taciturn aunt did not keep to herself. I had known since my early schooldays that I was a bastard. You learn about life in a rough fisher community and local gossip, rumour and insult had told me this much.

As I grew older the local people accepted me as the

poor do — I was not the only love-child fostered in the district, although in looks and temperament I was the strangest of them all.

William and Bessy Bawtry had brought me up in their little stone cottage overlooking The Quay for as long as I could remember. They called me their niece, and I knew they received a small amount of money each quarter day for my clothes and keep. But they told me nothing at all about my parents, or where I was born, except, as I have said, that my mother was a dancer, and this slipped out somehow when Bessy was in a temper with me over some forgetfulness or defiance and she left me in no doubt that to be a dancer's daughter was not at all a respectable thing to be.

'Tha'll learn soon enough when thou'rt older,' she would say in answer to my questioning, 'and happen thou'll not like it when tha' does knoa.'

With this I was supposed to be content. I was not, of course, and spun dreams about being a forgotten princess or a rich man's daughter and affected airs which made my school mates laugh behind their upheld pinafores.

'Lady Muck' they called me, and 'Black Bella Bawtry' — and their mothers said I was 'nowt but a gypsy brat, when all's said and done.' But the lads liked me, although they were rough as wild ponies, and I'd sooner be off with them over the cliffs than scrubbing floors or playing girls' games on the wide stone quayside.

When Bessy's daughter Janet left the chapel school she was put into service at Sutherdyke Hall, and her brother Tom began to help with the nets and lobster pots and go out with the fishing boats when he was barely twelve. But when I was too old for school I was sent for lessons to an elderly spinster who lived in the Old Town, whether to get me out of Aunt Bessy's way or to prepare me for some mysterious future, I did not know. When I questioned her she said I was no good in a house. I would be a fool at service. Perhaps I might be a governess, a school-teacher or a shop-lady. It was worth a few shillings, anyway, to keep me out of mischief and away from the lads who hung about the gate in the evening and whistled after my swinging plaits of straight black hair.

The lessons bored me and I longed to escape from the smells of lavender and old lady and from the small over-crowded room in which every movement of my long slim body seemed to sweep some petty treasure to the floor. If I did not want to go into service like poor Janet, working from dawn till dusk, bullied and patronised by the upper servants, I certainly did not want this.

Our part of Monkstonby was a huddle of stone fisher cottages hanging over the harbour like gulls' nests, a big old hotel and a new, red-brick Wesleyan Chapel. There was a new church, too, but that was where the crescents and esplanades were being laid out to the north of the town, and where the rich folk from the West Riding re-tired or came to spend the summer months. The Old Town, with the big priory church dating back to the Middle Ages, was a mile inland.

Sutherdyke was two miles northwards along the rising cliffs, and about half a mile from the sea. Every year the sea bit more of the land away in the fierce winter storms. They said whole villages had been eaten away in the past. Sutherdyke Hall, where Janet worked, was the nearest big house to Monkstonby, although there were many estates farther inland in the wolds. This East Riding country was good to farm, flat to plough, with wide cornfields and solid grey stone farmhouses standing in their windbreaks of closely planted trees, the sails of the cornmills spinning in the wind across the wide horizon.

Sutherdyke Hall and village and many hundreds of surrounding acres belonged to Sir Lockwood Broadbent.

7

Some years previously he had suffered a stroke from which he had never completely recovered. In his youth he had led a profligate life in London and abroad, and had become so notorious that local women would warn their sons 'watch out, lad, or tha'll end up like old Lockwood o' Sutherdyke — drunk and daft'. Sir Lockwood had even been preached against in chapel.

The house and estate were administered by his sister, Mrs. Somerby and her elder son, Mr. Dyson Somerby. I had seen Mrs. Somerby, a handsome lady of extreme elegance, shopping in the Old Town and driving in a carriage and pair. The younger Somerby boy, Courtney, was in the army, and was known locally as a 'reight chip off t'old block' and Janet, who saw him on his rare visits home, said he was very handsome and his mother doted upon him, and that the elder brother Dyson was 'a big chap, fair to work for, but a bit of a rough one for a gentleman born'. She had had occasional glimpses of Sir Lockwood and said he was always drunk and enough to scare the daylights out of anyone.

I was not supposed to go to the Hall to see Janet — another of my aunt's forbiddances which I did not obey. It would waste Janet's time, she said, and if she was called off her work to see me she would get into trouble. There was truth in this, but I did not care — I was lonely for Janet, my big sister and only friend. I used to go whenever I could, and sneak through the orchard to the kitchen yard. I would stand close to the wall, half-hidden by a water-butt and if Janet caught a glimpse of me she would creep out for a few minutes, and we would hug and exchange our brief and breathless news.

Sometimes in the summer and there was no one about we would sit hidden for a long time in the kitchen gardens, the air humming with bees, smelling of herbs and raspberries. In winter we would huddle in our shawls, the high rosy brick walls sheltering us from the east winds. Janet was four years older than I was and she would do anything for me. I was her little black baby, she said. She loved me and it gave me a sort of power over her.

On this particular Saturday I walked past the new villas with their poor little gardens struggling to exist in the stiff, spray-salt, easterly wind, along the sandy footpath, and up through the fields towards Sutherdyke. The great promontory of Norhead Point rose to the north, white cliffed, the breakers crashing against its foot. As I turned inland I could see the Hall miles away across the fields with the windows of the south-eastern front catching the rosy light of the afternoon sun. The wind was so stiff you could have leaned against it, and it plucked at my grey wool shawl as though it would blow me over the hedges. It is a fierce and dangerous coast. I have seen waves come over the harbour pier and break nearly to the top of Norhead Point where the lighthouse wings white and red throughout the night. William Bawtry could remember the great storm in the seventies, when the lifeboat was smashed to bits and a fleet of ships sunk in the North Sea. Forty poor drowned sailors lie in the priory church yard to prove it.

I went prudently about my errand, picking diligently along the hedgerows until the basket was nearly full of the black fruits, like the black, bead-headed clusters of pins they sell at the haberdashers' to pin ladies' veils.

The coachman's cottage was at the back of the stable yard and Mrs. Oldroyd, a stout busybody who had been in service at the Hall with my Aunt Bessy when they were girls, gave me some good cooking apples in exchange for the fish. She poured me some milk and cut a slice of lardy cake. She always eyed me curiously and I was sure she too knew something of my birth, but like my aunt, held her tongue.

'Still learning at Miss Alfriston's, Bella?' she asked, and I nodded, glowering at being reminded of my daily durance.

'Much good owt Miss Alfriston knows will do me or anyone.'

'Well, don't flash at me, Miss Temper! It's nowt of my doing.'

'It's a right waste of time I reckon. And money. Four shillings a week for that. I could learn it out of a book myself in ten minutes.'

'Aye, and wouldst thou?' Mrs. Oldroyd said, very rightly. 'I'd have put thee to service a year ago if I'd been your aunt. But she knows what she's doing, I dare say. Happen it'll come in one day.'

'Happen I'll run off wi' the gypsies and be a dancer like my mother.'

'Aye,' said Mrs. Oldroyd ironically, 'an' happen thy Uncle William'll give thee a strapping if he hears owt of that!'

I stared at her belligerently, hating her and all the grown-ups who told me nothing and imprisoned me in boredom. I was on the point of asking her, as I'd asked so many times at home, who was my mother and if she had known her? Had she really been a dancer? Was she, as some said, a sister of William Bawtry who had run off to London and got into trouble? Was I really misbegotten? Did anyone know who my father was? And where did I get my slim hands, my ivory skin and my long, straight black hair? Where did the money come from that was sent each quarter for my keep?

I knew it was no use asking. There was a conspiracy of secrecy or ignorance about me. Some did not know, some would not tell, some invented stories. I thanked her for the milk and cake and started on my way home.

I knew she would tell my aunt if I went into the stable-yard or through the wicket into the kitchen gardens to see Janet, so I went on until I was out of sight, then doubled back over a stile into the front paddock which lay between the house and the sea.

A balustrade ran along the edge of the ha-ha, with scantily-clad stone nymphs bearing fruit and flowers, looking cold in the east winds that blew from Monkstonby Bay. I crept along, dodging cow-pats and clumps of nettles. The wind whipped my waist-length plaits across my face and the grazing Herefords raised pied faces to watch.

Across the shaven lawns the big house of three storeys faced southward in the bend of the coast towards Norhead, so the seaward front always caught the sun and a big magnolia grandiflora climbed up to the roof, dropping petals from its huge white blossoms on to the grey paving of the south terrace, in the summer time.

The house had been refaced years ago, or so Miss Alfriston had told me, before the Queen was born, but she said the house was much older than that, and if you looked at the old walls, stables and the great beams in the kitchens you could see it was hundreds of years old. She could be quite interesting if I could get her to talk about local things and forget French verbs. The house had a huge and beautiful garden of trees and lawns. The rosegarden, famous throughout the county, and the flower beds, were on the inland side, sheltered from the sea.

I slipped through a gap in the hedge into the orchard, through the orchard into the kitchen yard, taking up my stance behind the water-butt, fixing my hopeful eyes on the back door.

From behind the stable wall I could hear the stamp of hooves, a groom whistling and the occasional clank of a pail. The clock on the coach house roof struck five and I knew I would have to go soon if I wanted to be home before dark.

The wicket gate leading to the kitchen garden opened cautiously, and Janet's fair head peered out. I was startled to see she was wearing a black dress, a white apron and a lace-edged cap pinned on to her curly fair hair. Usually she wore blue cotton and often a rough apron. She beckoned, and I raced across to her, and she pulled me behind the wicket gate and shut it. We hugged and kissed happily, for it was nearly two weeks since we had met.

'I can't stay but a minute,' she gasped. 'It's been a fair old muddle today. Mr. Courtney's home and brought company, and one of the housemaids is poorly, so I've been told to put on her blacks and help the butler. I've got to lay-up for him in a minute. Here — I've brought you this.'

'This' was a William pear, pale yellow, freckled and rosily flushed. I bit into it and the juice ran down my chin.

Janet asked after her parents and her brother. I gave her the news from The Quay, the bits of scandal, the scraps of gossip and happiness and bitterness that made up our lives. Tom had been taken on as regular boy on the *Seasprite*. There had been a big herring catch in the week and Uncle William had gone drinking. My aunt, fiercely Wesleyan and frugally saving, hated this and it had caused one of their periodic, violent quarrels. Janet was glad to be out of this — and so would I be too, but I had nowhere else to go.

I became aware that while we were talking she was staring at me in an intense and unusual way, her round blue-grey eyes taking in every detail of my face, and so presently I became self-conscious, and said sharply, 'What's to do? Is my face mucky, or summat?'

She flushed even pinker. 'Bella,' she said, and her eyes were so bright that I realised she was pink with excitement, not with running or the cold east wind on her cheeks. 'I went into the big dining-room for the first time today — I've always done t'servants' hall cleaning, washing t'crocks and suchlike. The butler took me along and showed me what I have to do to lay-up tonight, and, Bella — over the sideboard in t'dining-room there's a great picture of a lady, and it's the dead image o' thee, love.'

I thought I would choke with excitement and surprise. 'Never of *me*?'

'Aye, my little 'un, o' thee. Same hair and black eyes, same long neck and queer colouring.'

My skin is a creamy olive colour, it never chaps in the wind or burns in the sun and my cheeks never redden like Janet's. In hot summer weather I go brown, golden, not dusky like a gypsy — but I always look dark among the Monkstonby children with their Norse blood.

'It's a beautiful lady in a black lace gown, and a shawl embroidered with flowers, and jewels — and she standing on t'terrace here with t'ouse back of her, and she's the very spit of thee, Bella.'

'Can I see it? Take me there, Janet.'

'Eh, I'd be feared.'

'Just through t'window. I won't go in. Just a peep?'

'Nay, love, I dursn't.'

I had a power over her, she loved me and I always got my own way. I put my hands to my lips as though I was going to cry, although there was no need to pretend disappointment. If she had refused I would have cried. I longed to see the picture more than anything in the world.

'It's not the only one,' she said. 'There are lots of pictures of the same lady in that part of the house. One in the blue drawing-room, one in the hall . . .'

'Janet,' I was dancing with impatience, 'no one will see us. If they do I'll take all the blame. Janet . . .' a wild idea had come into my head, 'it might be my mother — it *might*!'

'Nay, it's a grand lady — thy mother was nowt but a stage dancer, or so folks say.' She hesitated. 'All right, then. Do as I say. If we see anyone, you must run back right away.'

'I promise, love. I promise — cross my heart!'

I put my basket down by the gate, and she took my hand and led me towards the house. The kitchen garden was a huge walled square which I learned, years later, had been part of of the tilt-yard where, in Queen Elizabeth's day the gentlemen jousted at the lists. We went along the brick paths between the lavender and rosemary bushes, behind the yellowing bean rows, under the hanging apple branches heavy with fruit, and out through another wicket on the far side, which opened on to a wide gravel walk at the side of the east wing. She pointed to the big front bay where three tall french windows looked out over the lawns and paddock to the sea.

'Yon's dining-room,' she whispered. 'T'window's open this side because I came out this road. We'll go inside for just a minute and out again reight sharp. Come now . . .'

I took her hand and we crept across the gravel walk, edged with dark yews. Janet pulled down the handle, pushed the window and, hardly breathing, we stepped into the big, beautiful room.

The lamps had already been lit and the table set and as I looked round I drew in my breath with amazement and delight. Did people really live in such places? I had never seen such a room or even imagined it could exist. Tapestries hung on the panelled walls, and gold-framed pictures. The long table was like a wide river of polished wood in which the blue glass lamps, silver, flowers and what looked like a waterfall of crystal drops hung from the moulded ceiling, were all reflected. Hepplewhite

14

chairs with slatted backs stood silently waiting the company, the carpets were of blue, of faded rose colours, amber and greens with leaves and ferns and flowers and shapes woven into them, and there was a tall wide chimney piece elaborately carved with scrolls and leaves and little people.

Janet took a silver candlestick on the polished sideboard and lifted it. 'Yon's t'picture, ower t'sideboard. That's her. Just go and have a look and then get thee off home.'

I took the candlestick from her hand and went nearer to the picture and stood gazing up at it, holding the light above my head.

It was true what Janet had said. It was the portrait of a very young woman with my clear, pale skin, my black sloe-shaped long-lashed eyes, my jet black hair, straight and long as Chinese hair. But the lady in the picture had her hair piled and looped into a chignon, coiled into ringlets on her neck, and she wore a little diadem. She had a tiny waist and was wearing a dress of black lace that seemed to drift across her beautiful shoulders, veiling rather than clothing her high young breasts. For all my chipped nails and broken cuticles my hands were like hers, long and narrow, with thin strong fingers, and nails shaped like almonds. But the hands in the portrait were weighted with gems and diamonds glittered in her ears and round her long, slender throat. Over one arm, hand on hip, she held the shawl that Janet had spoken of — white, long-fringed, smothered with embroidered flowers, and just below the hem of her skirt, which she lifted provocatively, showed a high-arched, thin, strong foot in a crimson shoe. She was standing on the terrace in a slanting sunset light, and the magnolia grandiflora was heavy with cream-coloured blooms. Her big, languorous eyes seemed to meet mine, and her full, soft red mouth

15

smiled with something of allure, something of self-mockery, something perhaps of boredom. She looked magnificent but not happy.

'But who is she?' I cried.

'Nay, how should I know? I never came in here before today.'

'There're some letters on the frame.' I craned forward, standing on tip-toe. 'I can't rightly see ... yes, now I can. Maria-Amata, it says ... that must be her name.'

Janet suddenly froze. There was a sound of dragging unsteady footsteps coming along the hall outside. I turned to put the candlestick down and run after Janet who had already reached the open window, but I was too late.

A tall, thin, wild-faced, elderly man came shuffling into the room. His hair was long-rusty grey, and looked uncared for, but in spite of his ravaged features and shaking hands there was a remnant of good looks and an air of quality about him. He was dressed in a long gown of dark silk, bound with a tasselled cord, shabby and stained. He wore no necktie and his linen did not look too clean. He came slowly across the room looking first at the portrait and then at me. A strong smell of spirits hung about him. I guessed it was Sir Lockwood Broadbent, the owner of this grand hall, the man who was rumoured mad and known never to be sober. I stood motionless like a hare in its form.

I heard Janet's whisper, telling me to run for it, but I could not move. I was tall for my age, even then; the red kerchief had fallen back — I suppose the likeness to the portrait was striking under the glow of the candles.

Janet found her courage, came to my side, took the candlestick from my nerveless hand.

'Come away. It's t'owd meister. He's drunk as ever — he'll not remember, like as not. Bella, *come*!' But as I moved, he shouted loudly and suddenly, 'Stay!'

I caught a glimpse of myself in the mirror opposite, the

portrait behind me. The likeness *was* uncanny. He staggered forward, dropped on his knees, his hands clutching at my kersey skirts and I shrieked and ran down the room towards the open window.

'Maria,' he cried, as though in agony. 'Maria-Amata, don't go. In Christ's name stay . . . I cannot live without you. Maria-Amata stay with me . . .'

He dragged himself to his feet, stumbling down the long lovely room, falling against chairs, sending pieces of china and silver crashing, coming towards me with those pleading, shaking, terrifying claws outstretched, his mouth working, his eyes wild with a terrifying glare of hope, incredulous despairing hope.

'This time you are real,' he cried. 'This is not delirium. I am in hell without you and I will not let you go again . . .'

He reached out, and as he did so he fell full length, clutching my skirts so tightly that I could not escape. As he fell he began to make a horrible noise in his throat, and his eyes, which were a transparent, startling blue, rolled upwards. He seemed convulsed with some kind of fit.

The noise of the falling furniture and breaking china must have aroused the house, but now I screamed for Janet at the top of my voice. She came loyally to my side, and we stood looking fearfully down at the twisting figure at my feet. Footsteps came racing along the hall outside, and Hawkins, the butler, burst into the room followed by two men in evening dress, an unusually tall, broad-shouldered man with a serious, blunt-featured face, and one of the handsomest boys I had ever seen. Even in my state of paralysed fear I was aware of him, of his grace, his bright hair and his eyes, with their azure irises, transparent as blue glass.

The tall young man knelt by Sir Lockwood, calling his

name, then said, 'It's a seizure. Mother has been afraid of this. Courtney, get a carriage and drive into Monkstonby to the doctor. Bring him back with you. I'll take Sir Lockwood to his room.'

He bent to lift the recumbent man whose hand still held my skirt in a vicelike grip. He prised the fingers gently open. I let out a gasp of relief and turned to fly.

'Stay where you are!' he said, sharp and hard, as a man speaks to a dog, and for the first time really looked at me. Then slowly he turned his glance to the portrait over the sideboard and then back to me. Courtney stared too and said, 'What's this? A gypsy brat after the silver?'

'No,' I cried out, 'I did not come to steal.'

'Why did you come then?'

'Courtney,' his brother said, 'there is no time for questions. Go and get the doctor. The child will stay until I can see her. Get on your way.'

He went, but even on so urgent a message I could see he resented taking orders from his brother. The big man, who was the elder brother, Dyson Somerby, lifted his uncle like a feather, the ravaged face, contused and red, fell against his shoulder. The wild eyes were fixed and blind.

'Stay here,' he said. 'Both of you. Come with me, Hawkins.'

He carried his uncle out of the room. Janet and I burst into tears, noisy at first, and then quietening as time passed, and we stood there, not daring to go or to sit down on any of the satin-covered chairs, and only speaking in whispers.

'Is he dead, d'you think?'

'Will they send for the police?'

'D'you think they'll beat me?'

To all of which Janet replied in monosyllables, shaking her head, holding my hand in her work-roughened hand, her arm about my shoulder, sometimes saying, 'Nay, nay, don't cry, my little love. We've done nowt wrong.'

It seemed hours and the sun had set before Mr. Somerby returned. He was a fine figure of a man, broad and immensely tall, a real sturdy Yorkshire man. His eyes were grey with thick light brown lashes, and his light brown hair was cut short. He had a square freckled face, with a big firm-lipped mouth that looked as though it was hard for him to smile. There were freckles on the backs of his big, well-shaped hands. He looked down at us and we clung closer together. He spoke to the butler.

'Now, what is all this?'

'This is Bawtry.' Hawkins indicated Janet. 'She is one of the kitchen maids. She has always been a good girl, sir, and as the parlourmaid is ill, Mrs. Shawncliffe told her to help me this evening.'

'And who is the other — the dark one?'

Hawkins shrugged. He was not a local man. 'She comes to see Bawtry, sir. I thought it was her sister.'

'Well,' barked Mr. Somerby, 'are you her sister?'

'No, sir.'

'Well, what are you?'

'Please, sir, I don't know . . .' and I burst into tears.

Janet held me close, and said, 'She's lived wi' us since she was a baby. She's like a sister. It's my fault, sir. I hadn't been in this part o' t'ouse until today, and when I saw the picture there, it was so like, I told Bella, and she wanted to see it, so I brought her in to see it, and just as we were going t'owld . . . that is, the meister came, and he went mad or something, kept calling her Maria Amata, and trying to catch her . . .'

Mr. Somerby put out a big freckled hand, took my chin and turned my face up to the lights. His hand was cool and smelled pleasantly of lavender.

'Yes,' he said, 'there is no doubt of the likeness. What is your name, child?'

'Isabel. Bella Bawtry, they call me, though Aunt Bessy is not my mother, nor Uncle Bawtry my father.' I glared at him, for I was finding my courage, and my temper started to spark at his attitude. I was not a stray puppy to be examined and discussed. 'My mother was a dancer, and I don't know who my father was. No one will tell me.'

There was a commotion in the hall, voices, footsteps and flying rustle of silk. Mrs. Somerby came quickly into the room calling her son.

'Dyson ... come quickly. The doctor has not arrived yet and I think your uncle is dying ...' She stopped, changed colour, staring at me.

'Did you know about this child, Mother?'

'Of course.'

'Has nothing been done for her?'

'I send a small amount for her keep each quarter.'

'Why did you not tell me?'

'Good heavens,' she cried, 'if I told you of half your uncle's follies about the county we would run a foundling home.'

He looked at her gravely and there was antagonism between them as though he never quite believed what she said. She glanced at Hawkins, as though reminding him of the man's presence, and cried urgently, 'Dyson, you *must* come upstairs ... I believe your uncle is dying ...' There was the sound of a door opening and voices in the hall. 'Thank God, there is Courtney back with the doctor ...' She went from the room, and Dyson said to Hawkins, 'Tell Oldroyd to drive this child back to her home while he is waiting for the doctor and send Bawtry back to the kitchen. Then you must take the trap and inform our guests. There will be no dinner-party tonight.'

He went out. As Hawkins hustled us out through the great hall, which went right up to the roof, all panelled and emblazoned, I saw Courtney with Mr. Somerby and the doctor going up the wide oaken staircase. Janet, giving me just a scared glance of farewell, scuttled through a baize-lined door leading to the servants' quarters, and I was marched out through the main entrance, where Oldroyd, whom I knew, was waiting with the carriage for the doctor's return. He stared when Hawkins said he was to drive me to Monkstonby.

'My basket,' I wailed. 'My blackberries and t'apples Mrs. Oldroyd gave me, Aunt Bessy'll skin me if I go back wi'out them.'

Hawkins went back into the house, dissociating himself from me, but Oldroyd went to the kitchen garden and retrieved my basket and we set off home. I had never ridden in a carriage before — a little, warm, leather-padded room, with the clop of the horses' hooves ahead, and the dark countryside flashing past the windows. I examined everything. The blind tassels, the pockets edged with braid, the net for parcels. I bounced up and down on the upholstery like the child I was. I thought of the lady in the picture, whom I was now quite sure was my mother, and imagined that I was really a princess. Then I remembered Sir Lockwood, and his look of frantic longing, not like love, as though he would devour me ... and was afraid again. Was he dead? Was it my fault? Would that make me a murderer? Would they lock me up in the bailey in the Old Town and haul me off to York to prison in the morning? I would have to tell Aunt Bessy. I began to cry in the dark to myself.

I got out of the carriage at the top of the cobbled lane and ran down to the cottage on the harbour side and let myself in as quietly as I could. Oldroyd drove off again with a clatter of turning hooves.

Bessy heard me and called, 'Now where'st tha bin, tha little devil? Out wi' lads? Come in here this minute and leave thy clogs under t'sink.' I did as I was bid, pattering over her spotlessly scrubbed floor in my stocking feet.

I put my basket on the table, where she was sitting sewing by the lamp. I did not want to tell her, because this was one of her rare happy hours. The blustering wind had dropped, her husband and her lad were out with the boats on a safe sea, the house was clean and shining, smelling sweetly of her afternoon's baking and under her little white cap her square heavy face bent over her sewing, so peaceful, good and simple. But not tonight. It was after dark, and I was over two hours late. She looked at me and said, 'Well, what's to do, then?'

And so, between sobs and with many pleading glances I told her what had happened, and she listened without a word, and when I had finished, I ventured, 'It's my mother, isn't it? The woman in the picture in the fine clothes? Was he my father — owld Sir Lockwood?' She nodded. 'Then I am a bastard? Like they've always said?'

'Aye. I said tha wouldn't like it when tha learned.' She nodded to the chair before me. 'Sit thee down.'

'But he's a gentleman,' I cried. I pulled the chair out, and sat down, leaning across towards her, wanting to shake her out of her calmness. My head was awhirl with dreams. I was misbegotten, as I had always known, but my father was a baronet who owned a great estate and my mother was a beautiful lady. 'Tha said she was a dancer,' I said accusingly, 'but the picture is of a grand lady in jewels and lace.'

'She were a dancing girl from Spain,' she said bluntly, picking up her sewing again as though hemming the cuff of the calico shirt made everything she said ordinary and acceptable. A dancing girl from Spain. If she had said the

22

Empress of China it could not have been more extraordinary to me.

'A dancer from Spain,' I repeated incredulously.

'Aye, a foreigner.' As she said this she looked up at me, as though the fact itself was past belief. I thought so too. The only foreigners I had ever seen were the foreign fishermen who on rare occasions brought their boats into shelter from the North Sea gales. Froggies we called them all wherever they came from.

'Sir Lockwood was a reight bad 'un all his life, then at fifty he lost his head over this young lass from Spain. I don't think he was right in his head from the moment he saw her.'

'Tell me, tell me!' I banged impatiently on the table.

She told me what she knew. It was a fantastic story, although at thirteen the despair of a passionate obsession escaped me. Escaped her too. In her hard-working life bounded by the danger of the sea, poverty and narrow religion, what did she know of such a case and such people? Their excesses were beyond her understanding — to her they were daft, and so she told me.

Sir Lockwood had rarely been at Sutherdyke all through his youth and manhood. Old Lady Broadbent, his mother, had been widowed early and although he was her only son, they quarrelled bitterly. When he came into his inheritance he lived a life of pleasure in London and Europe and never married, and he was fifty when he met the Spanish dancer. She was very young, she was a flamenco dancer and had become a great star of the Parisian music halls. She toured all the great capitals of Europe. She was pursued by rich men, written about in newspapers, photographed, fêted and adored. Maria-Amata Hernandez — La Belle Amata they called her.

She became Sir Lockwood's mistress. He followed her round Europe, spending a fortune on her. Carriages, clothes, jewels, furs, parties, flowers. But when she was eighteen she became pregnant and he brought her to Sutherdyke. His mother left the house and went to live with her daughter, Mrs. Somerby, and never spoke to him again.

'Eh, he was daft,' said Bessy, shaking her head over her sewing. 'Right cracked in t'ead. It was said she was in love with some young fellow, a dancer, and that Sir Lockwood had him killed but I don't know the truth of it. He was mad enough for owt. He would give that lass anything or do anything just to keep her by his side, and she wanted nowt but to get away from him. He was scared when the baby — that was you — when the baby came she'd be off again on to the stage. She was never well at Sutherdyke. She came from a place she called Andalucia, where it was hot.'

Bessy said Hernandez and Andalucia with the Spanish lisp as she must have heard Maria-Amata say it years ago, although Spain was as distant as the moon to her and its inhabitants three-headed for all she knew.

'But I am his daughter,' I said, drawing myself up, my eyes flashing. 'Why did he send me here? Why didn't he come to see me? Or let me have some money?'

'I said not to get ideas,' said Bessy crushingly. 'Tha'st not t'only one in these parts as is born on wrong side o' t'blanket and I reckon more than one o' them is owld Sir Lockwood's. Tha's had more than most. Mrs. Somerby always sent money — not much but regular. You should be grateful for that.'

I was not grateful. I sat there fuming. I was not proud of him. The reeling, drunken figure clutching despairingly at my skirts had sickened me. But I did come from great folk as I had always dreamed, and if my mother was not a princess she had been famous and beautiful. That was enough to set my head awhirl.

'What happened to my mother?' I demanded. 'Is she dead? Did he kill her too?'

'Aye, in a way — killed her wi' love. After you were born she ran off, as he had feared, left everything he'd given her and went off back to her dancing. I'd just had our Tom, so t'housekeeper called me in as wet-nurse — a little black thing tha wast. Sir Lockwood went off after Maria, followed her all over Europe, they said. But she was ill, too ill to dance, and when he found her he brought her back again to Sutherdyke to die.'

She stopped sewing for a moment and sighed.

'She used to sit in t'rose-garden looking at photograph pictures of herself and old bits out t'newspaper about her. It was like a blight on a flower seeing her lovely arms get thin, and her great dark eyes sink into her bonny face. She hated Sutherdyke. She was never warm, sitting huddled up in furs all day, and she hated him for keeping her there. She'd nobbut a few words of English. "Mwee frio," she'd say, "mwee frio" like a lapwing mewing. Cold, very cold. She never wanted a child. She would look at thee as though tha were a kitten, and say "Mwee wappa" — which means very pretty in her tongue, and turn away. She used to dance sometimes, rattling them castanets and drumming with her heels as you never saw the like, holding her head very proud and fierce. She'd dance until she'd cough, and cough until she could not stand, and in spite of all the doctors, and taking her to Harrogate and Scarborough, she died. If she had gone to her own country 'appen it would have been better, but Sir Lockwood would not take her in case she never came back. So she died and he went fair out o' his mind. They had to lock him up or he'd never have let them bury her. He drank all the time. He would not look at you, or have you in the house. Said you'd killed her. Mrs. Somerby came and took over running the house, for she was a

25

widow by then and none too well off, and she told me to tek thee home here and she'd send money. And that's how it's been ever since.'

'If he loved Amata like that, why didn't he marry her?'

Aunt Bessy looked at me with her sober look, and said, 'She was nobbut a dancer, love. An actress, after all. You couldn't expect it.'

I felt utterly desolate — all my fine dreams collapsing about me. I did not belong here in this cottage with these good, rough people, and I did not belong at Sutherdyke Hall. There was no place for me anywhere. I said, out of my misery, 'What's to become of me?'

'I went and asked Mrs. Somerby, when you were ten and too old for t'school, and she said to send you to Miss Alfriston for more learning. Get a bit of refinement, she said, then 'appen she'd get you summat, lady's maid or a shop place . . . or if you were clever at books, a governess. So don't go getting any grand ideas. Expect nowt from the Broadbents because nowt is what you'll get. So now tha knowst and I hope tha's satisfied.'

I was not — I was seething with resentment. I could not sleep. I was filled with wild plans to storm up to Sutherdyke and demand some kind of recognition. I was Sir Lockwood's daughter, and he had no other children, or none known, for all my aunt's surmising. I thought of Mrs. Somerby and her two sons, the presumed heirs of Sutherdyke, and was filled with sullen anger against them.

The next morning we heard that Sir Lockwood was dead of a stroke. Bessy went to the funeral in the little church at Sutherdyke, as many people did from all over the country, but she would not take me. I had caused enough trouble, she said.

The days went by, lessons at Miss Alfriston's, helping at the cottage or at the stall where Bessy sold fish on market days, gutting and scaling with her knobby red hands. I brooded and dreamed and resented my fate. It was all very well for Bessy to accept things as they were but not me. I thought of my mother, her fame and beauty and the men who had loved her and I wanted to know all about her. I wanted to be like her. To be a lady, or a proud dancer, famous and desired. But to go into service! To get a position as a governess or in a shop, to marry a local lad and spend my life scrubbing floors—! I decided I would not. I would die first. I would run away to London or with the gypsies.

Then one day when I came back from Miss Alfriston's I saw the Sutherdyke carriage standing at the top of the cobbled alley, with Oldroyd on the box. I imagined he must be waiting for Mrs. Somerby who might be doing some shopping in the district, but when I went in to the back kitchen, Bessy called to me to take off my clogs and come into the parlour. We never used the cold little room with the crinkled red paper round the fireplace, and the chenille table cloth edged with bobbles on which stood the family Bible and a treasured aspidistra. Bessy was sitting at the table with Uncle William, both of them very stiff and solemn, and opposite them sat Mr. Dyson Somerby, his big body in its caped broadcloth overcoat obliterating the tiny chair and filling the room, his tall hat on the table. Beside him on an equally uncomfortable chair sat a pleasant elderly man and on the table was a legal-looking case with a lot of papers. Both the men rose at my entrance, and although I was a tall girl for thirteen, I felt small. But I did feel important — for the first time in my life.

'Is this the young lady?' asked the pleasant elderly man, extending his hand.

'Yes.' Mr. Somerby introduced me, referring to me as Isabel. I had been called Bella as long as I could remember.

'This is Mr. Shawcross, my late uncle's solicitor.'

The old gentleman shook my hand politely. My knees began to knock.

'The likeness is absolutely astonishing,' he said. 'Without, of course, the enchanting little foreign ways . . .'

'Quite,' said Mr. Somerby shortly. 'I think you'd better tell her, Mrs. Bawtry.'

I looked at Bessy. Wildly it crossed my mind that they were going to bring some accusation against me for Sir Lockwood's death.

'Sit thee down, Bella love.'

I did as I was bid.

'It seems, Bella, that we've been on t'wrong road, thinking you misbegotten. Mr. Somerby has found documents proving Sir Lockwood and your mother were married.'

'In Vienna,' said Mr. Shawcross. 'Eight months before you were born. When Mr. Somerby went through his uncle's effects he found your mother's jewel case, and both your birth certificate and the marriage certificate had been locked away in it all these years. Indeed it was most admirable of Mr. Somerby . . .'

Mr. Somerby stirred, and said impatiently, 'Shawcross, don't chatter. Let's get the business over and done with.'

I clung to the table edge, feeling as though I might keel over on to the floor. I must have looked awful for Mr. Shawcross asked my aunt to get me some water and told me to sit down.

'There's nothing to be frightened of. You are a very lucky young lady.'

'But what does it mean?'

'It means that you are the legitimate daughter of Sir Lockwood and Lady Broadbent, and when you are twenty-one you will inherit his estate.'

'But does it mean Sutherdyke and all that belongs to

me? And I can ride in a carriage and have a pony and wear silk on a Sunday?'

Dyson Somerby gave a short bark of laughter. I did not know then or understand what his discovery had meant to the Somerbys. But for me, the estate would have gone to Mrs. Somerby and thence to her sons, for Sir Lockwood had made no will.

'It will mean all that,' said Dyson, 'and a great deal more. At the moment, as I administer my uncle's estates and have done for some years, Mr. Shawcross and myself have been made your guardians. You will come to live at Sutherdyke, it is your home. And we must find something rather better than Miss Alfriston's in the way of school.'

I thought he was stiff and forbidding. I did not like the idea of more school.

'Then won't I have a pony of my own and a silk dress for Sundays?' I cried. 'Nay, if I'm to get nowt but lessons I can't see owt grand in being a lady.'

A light flickered in the hard grey eyes and he rubbed his long upper lip with his thumbnail, concealing his mouth. I did not think he was suppressing laughter. I did not think he ever laughed.

'It will mean all that and more,' he said soberly. 'One day you will inherit a great estate. You must learn to be worthy of it. It will not be easy. My mother and brother are not pleased by this discovery and I am not welcoming the responsibility of a young lass. But here you are and something must be done about you. It is our plain duty. I will arrange for you to come over to live in your house in Sutherdyke.'

With that somewhat frosty welcome he turned and strode out of the house. Mr. Shawcross shook my hand, tutted a bit, seemed to be about to say something else, changed his mind and followed Mr. Somerby.

I stood aglow with delight, not knowing what to say.

Bessy returned from showing them out. We heard the carriage clatter away.

'I'd best get thy clothes together,' she said, then, thoughtfully, 'That Mr. Dyson Somerby is a rare one. I reckon he could have burned them papers, and no one would have known a thing about you. You'd have stopped here all your life.'

'He must be made of iron, I reckon,' said William, speaking for the first time. I stared at them uncomprehendingly. I was already spinning dreams, and prominent in those dreams was the graceful, bright-haired boy with the insolent manner and azure blue eyes ... the younger brother. The chip 'off t'owld block'. Courtney Somerby.

CHAPTER TWO

It was arranged that I should go to Sutherdyke Hall the following week and that a carriage was to be sent for me. All my excited anticipation of splendour returned and I tried to pretend I was not frightened out of my wits. Bessy kept her counsel as usual, but I told Miss Alfriston and soon the story was all over the parish. My following of fisher lads suddenly kept a respectful distance and people who had never noticed me or considered themselves above me became very affable. Invitations to tea came from the mothers of girls who had not been allowed to speak to me before. Bessy set her mouth and refused them all. It was for *them* she said (meaning the Somerbys) not *her* to decide whom I should and should not know.

She fussed around packing my little box, seeing that every poor article of clothing that I possessed was clean, pressed and mended. She took away my clogs and holland apron. 'Nay, tha'll not need them, love,' she said, and in saying this put a barrier of class between us in a way that made me sad and proud, for there had never been a day when I had not worn an apron, a coarse one at week-ends, a linen one on Sundays — it was the stamp of a cottage girl. We were never to be on the same side of that barrier again.

'I'll never forget thee, Aunt Bessy. And when I come into my money I'll buy thee a satin dress wi'bugle beads. And I'll come to see thee every week.'

'Eh, well, we'll see,' she said. 'Happen tha will change.

Better if tha does change, or it will be a waste of time and money, for tha'st a reight rough tongue for a lady.' She smiled bleakly at what was as near a joke as she found possible.

I was to go to Sutherdyke Hall in my best blue dress and red flannel petticoat, my Sunday shawl which was not knitted but of good West Riding cloth with a blue check woven into it, and my Sunday boots which had been handed down when Janet grew too big for them.

Uncle William hardly spoke to me, but when he did he watched his language and never raised a hand however wild and saucy I became in my excitement. Young Tom Bawtry stared at me with round blue eyes, and rubbed his curly head, muttering exclamations of incredulity.

'Well, Our Bella, a lady up at Sutherdyke Hall! It beats cock-fighting. I'd never have thowt it. That Mrs. Somerby'll be thy aunty then? Eh, I reckon tha'll forget all about us and ride past with thy mucky nose in the air.'

In the end I hit out at him and we wrestled and shrieked with laughter, until Bessy got cross and said that all the brass in the world would never make a lady out of me. But beneath all this we were tense and anxious and when the men went off down the harbour side Bessy said soberly, 'It won't be easy, Bella. There'll be a lot to learn, and tha'st no patience for learning. But if it turns out bad, tha canst always come back here. As long as we're alive there'll always be a home here. Will told me to tell you that.' And at that I burst into tears and flung my arms round her neck. She released my clinging arms and went to her drawer where she kept a few family papers, and took out a small packet in yellowed paper. It rattled as she moved it.

'Tha'd best have these now.'

I stared at the objects. Four pieces of hollowed black

32

wood, fastened into pairs with tasselled cords of yellow and red.

'But what are they?'

'Castanets — or so thy mother called them. She gave them to me years ago.'

'But what are they for?'

'To make a noise when she was dancing. Like this.' She pulled the cord over her work-worn finger and laboriously made a clicking sound. I put the other on my right hand and my long supple fingers made it clatter. 'Aye, like so. She could make them talk — whisper, or growl, or shout ... whatever she liked. You tek them. It's all I have of hers. Off to bed now. It'll be a new life for thee in t'morning.'

So I slept for the last time in the little room which I had had to myself since Janet went into service. The thought that she was at Sutherdyke was a comfort to me — at least there would be one familiar face.

The thick-walled cottage had been my home all my life. It was damp, and in spite of Bessy's scrubbing and scouring, always smelled faintly of fish from the lock-up where William kept lobster pots and nets, and where she gutted the fish she sold along the quayside. I watched the stars move across the small, square window in the thick walls and wondered if I would ever sleep there again.

The carriage came for me promptly at two o'clock. There had been an early frost, but it was a lovely day as we bowled out of the town and northward along the Sutherdyke Road. I felt very grand. The carriage had stopped at the top of the cobbled alley and the uniformed coachman had carried my little wooden box up the donkey steps and put it beside him on the driving-seat, opened the door, handed me in, and covered my knees with a rug. It was a landau, and he asked me if I would like the hood raised or preferred it left open. It was the second time in my life I had ridden in a carriage and the first time I had been asked to give an order. I blushed bright red and told him to leave the hood as it was and sat up very stiff and proud because a small crowd of our neighbours had gathered, And I remembered how the children had laughed behind their pinnies at my dreams of grandeur.

Oldroyd, the husband of Bessy's friend, was a middle-aged man, very smart in his cord breeches and highly polished leggings, a hard square hat on his greying head. I had often met him when I had taken messages to his wife, so the minute we were out of town I sprang over to the front seat, and leaning over the panel, chatted to him as he drove. He glanced down from the box a little uncomfortably, not quite knowing how to address me. But I had no such reticences. I was not afraid of Oldroyd and I wanted to know everything I could about Sutherdyke and the Somerbys. I fired a barrage of questions. Mr. Dyson Somerby he told me had had charge of Sir Lockwood's affairs since he was a young man just out of college. He was a great man of business . . . folk said he could make a fortune on his own, if he wanted, but felt he had a duty to his uncle. Mr. Courtney, the lieutenant, was more like his uncle, a real good-looker, a 'reight young devil' more like the Broadbents than the Somerbys, but maybe foreign service would do him good.

I sat down on my heels in dismay.

'He's going away?'

'Aye, he's off to India with the regiment. Matter of weeks now.'

That bright, swift, graceful presence had been the one vivid attraction at Sutherdyke. He looked down at me and smiled at my undisguised disappointment.

'There's more lasses than thee will be upset, Bella, and his mother's breaking her heart.'

'Did you ever see *my* mother?'

34

'The Spanish lady?' he asked cautiously.

'Sir Lockwood's wife,' I said fiercely. 'Lady Broadbent.'

He looked at me under his thick grey eyebrows. The rumours of my legitimacy must have spread to Sutherdyke. He hesitated, then asked his only question, 'It's right, then, what we've been hearing? That you're the meister's legal daughter?'

'Yes. It's right. Tell me about my mother. Was she beautiful?'

Oldroyd swallowed nervously.

'I reckon she was more than that, miss,' he said. 'I reckon them as saw her would never forget her.'

That 'miss' accepted me as one of the family. The family was Oldroyd's world. If the family accepted me, then Oldroyd would give me unquestioning loyalty and service. I had never been addressed so before and my heart swelled with pride.

The carriage drove through the gates, along the drive and drew up before a pillared portico with a big triangular pediment. I was handed down, my box whisked away, and the butler, the dreaded Mr. Hawkins, took charge of me. He must have recognised me as the frightened gypsy lass of the night of Sir Lockwood's death, but he gave no sign and preserved his impenetrable air of condescension. I thought his Cockney voice indicated some superiority, having heard no other accent but my native Yorkshire. As he led me through the hall I gazed in awe at the panelled walls and moulded ceiling, the great oriel with its emblazoned glass overlooking the drive. There were family portraits, two of my mother, weapons polished and arranged in patterns, and a long refectory table of great age. He opened a door into a room in the opposite wing to the dining-room and told me to go in.

It was an exquisite room. The walls were white, like

miré silk, and the ceiling was painted blue with stars and clouds and little naked boys. The heavy curtains were of blue brocade and the carpets were blue and rose, and there were cabinets full of china, blue with white raised figures, and a lot of satin-covered chairs. There was a bright fire burning behind a glass shield, and in the window bay a huge screen with flowers and Chinamen and birds and trees and little castles all worked in gold.

Over the hearth was another portrait of Maria-Amata, a head and shoulder study, with her hair about her shoulders, against a background of patterned blue tiles. As Janet had said, there were very many portraits of my mother in the house.

'It's like heaven!' I gasped.

'This 'ere is the blue drawing-room,' said Hawkins. 'If you will wait I will acquaint Mr. Somerby of your arrival, young woman.'

He turned towards the door with a kind of ponderous mince, or mincing ponderousness, and for the life of me I could not help swaying along behind him in unison with his fat behind. When he turned I bent quickly over the table examining a book of flower prints. He looked at me suspiciously before he went out.

There was a burst of laughter and Courtney Somerby stepped out from behind the lacquered screen at the end of the room and came towards me. He was dressed formally in a frock coat of dark broadcloth and finely checked trousers. He was so handsome, so well-groomed and beautifully dressed that his elegance made me conscious of what I was by training if not by birth — a common fisher lass. I thrust my hands behind me so he should not see their cracked nails. I stared up, red-faced, into eyes which were alight with mischief. I became acutely conscious of my thick best boots.

'That take-off of old Hawkins wasn't half bad, brat!'

36

He moved round me, examining me critically, as though he were buying a horse. 'Must have a bit of the theatre in you from your mother.'

I knew he was baiting me and I felt my temper begin to rise. He looked critically at the picture of Maria-Amata and then down at me. 'You're not as good-looking, you're so skinny. But there's certainly a likeness. I wonder if my uncle was really your father — as Dyson insists.'

He bent and put his face so near mine that our noses almost touched. His eyes seemed enormous pools of blue. 'She hasn't a tongue,' he said.

'I have that and a sight more civil than thine!' I struck at him blindly, trembling with love and fury.

'Whoa!' He backed away, delighted that he had drawn me. I hated being thirteen, thin and shapeless, hated my clothes and my rough accent. I wanted him to admire me and I loathed myself for standing there like a 'great gaup wi' nowt to say.'

'She has a Spanish temper too! Or perhaps a Broadbent temper, for they have tempers, though Dyson controls his to bursting point and Mama's has declined into a mere wail of protest. But my uncle had a famous temper. Perhaps Dyson is right about you. There's a dashed fierce look of old Lockwood about you.'

Then, as though tired of the game, he threw himself petulantly into an arm-chair — a mixture of extreme sophistication and boyish wilfulness that was beyond my understanding. I was fascinated.

'She can't expect the Somerbys to like her. Until a month ago we merely knew she existed somewhere — one of Uncle Lockwood's little byeblows. Now — suddenly, there she is, standing on the hearthrug, smouldering away with great dark eyes and apparently with more right than we have to be there! It's quite ridiculous.'

'I canna help it,' I said. He was as handsome as an

angel, yet sullen as a petted boy of my own age. 'I don't want to tek anything from thee, lad. Why can't we just share it all? Everything. You can have half of everything that belongs to me.'

He stared at me in astonishment.

'Why on earth should she do that?'

'I told thee I don't want to take anything away from thee.'

'I believe she would,' he said incredulously, 'upon my soul I can't understand why.'

I could not express my feelings. For his mother and brother I had no thought. Only for him.

'I want thee to have everything tha want. Can't I sign some papers or summat to give thee half? I'll tell Mr. Somerby and Mr. Shawcross that I'll do it and gladly. Only ... only ...' I could hardly bring the words out. 'Only don't call me she, mister, as though I weren't there.'

I think it was at that moment he first realised that he had caught me. Standing there, shivering in my thick boots, my eyes and cheeks ablaze with admiration and dawning love.

'Well, well, well,' he smiled. 'I wish that it was as simple as that, brat. I wish dry-as-dust Dyson would agree with you. When you are twenty-one you can do just that — but that's eight years away. I might be dead in eight years,' at the thought of such a catastrophe, my childish heart contracted with pain, 'and besides I want to do a lot of living in the next eight years or so. I should be nearly thirty then ... getting old.'

'Didn't Sir Lockwood' — I could not bring myself to say my father. The name brought back that crazy, clawing death, so vividly. 'Did not Sir Lockwood leave you anything?'

'Oh, yes.' He took a golden case from his pocket and lit a thin black cigar. 'Oh, yes.' Everything he possessed was expensive and beautifully made. 'He made settlements on Mother and myself and Dyson when we first came to live here — about five hundred pounds a year each.'

'But that's a great deal of money.' I thought of William and Bessy and the meagre amount that kept their poor household.

'Not to me, brat. But there is nothing we can do now, since Dyson insists on the letter of the law. Had we known about you before my uncle's death I might have done something.' He looked up at me, the light catching the transparent blue irises of his eyes making him look as wickedly innocent as the cherubs on the ceiling. 'Such as pushing you into the harbour on a dark night.'

'I can swim,' I said. 'Tha'd have had to knock me ower t'head first.'

'Coarsely said but true. What sound common sense you have.'

'I reckon thou'rt too fine a gentleman for such work.'

'I could have hired one of the gentry that hang around The Crown at Norhead.' It was an inn with an evil reputation at Norhead village, some five miles away. 'Or one of the villains from the docks at Hull. I don't suppose it would cost much.' He watched me closely and I returned his gaze steadily. He was not going to catch me out again. He burst out laughing. 'You didn't take me seriously, did you?'

I laughed too, and shook my head, relieved, not because I had believed his nonsense, but because I so passionately wanted him to like me.

'What's your name?' he asked.

'Isabel Maria Bawtry. They call me Bella Bawtry. Happen I'm Isabel Maria Broadbent now.'

'Well, Isabel, if you're going to be a lady you must not say 'appen when you mean I suppose.'

And I, who would flash fire at any criticism with the

touchy temper of adolescence, said humbly, 'I will try if tha pleases.'

'And you must drop these tha's and thee's. It sounds like a damned Quaker meeting.'

'I will try.'

I longed for his approval, the young elegant, lounging there like an indolent royalty, but his mood changed as abruptly as cloud shadows on the moors. The sullen unhappy look came back into his eyes.

'Don't trouble to please *me*! Dyson is the one you must please. He has control over the money bags. And my mother, who is the social arbiter here at Sutherdyke. She invites all the rich local girls, hoping I will marry one — Yorkshire puddings the lot of them. Anyway, I shall only be here for a short while. I'm being shipped off to India with my regiment.'

The bottom fell out of my world as I remembered this.

'Soldiers get furlough,' I said.

'Only soldiers with money can afford to come home from India,' he said. 'Neither my brother nor Mr. Shawcross will let me have sufficient money out of the estate to live like a gentleman.' His beautiful face held an expression of despair. 'Army life in England is unutterably boring without money and India will be hell. They might as well send me to jail for six years.'

'I'll be nineteen in six years.'

'So you will,' he said indifferently, and then looked up at the portrait. 'Your mother was nineteen when that was painted.'

'Did you ever see her?'

'I saw her once. My mother brought me here to ask for money. We were always coming to ask my uncle for more money. I was about seven, I suppose. We were shown in here by mistake, and Maria-Amata was dancing by herself in the firelight. She was exquisite, like no other woman

I have ever seen. Although I was so young I understood my uncle's passion for her. But she was so thin, emaciated, a ghost dancer. You know they say she haunts the rose-garden here.'

'I've heard so.'

'Old women's tales. She was in white, her hair about her shoulders. She just looked at us with her great dark sad eyes, and my mother hurried me out of the room. My mother never spoke to her, or allowed her to be mentioned, because of course everyone thought she was the old man's mistress then.' He laughed ironically. 'Not that it would have made any difference if we had known about the marriage. She was a dancer, not a respectable person.'

He stood up, throwing his cigar into the fire, still looking at the picture.

'You must not think because the house is full of pictures of her that we accepted her. My uncle had her painted by all the best men — the pictures are valuable now. I wish they were mine to sell.'

'I'd sell t'lot tomorrow and give thee — give *you* the money,' I burst out passionately, and he began to laugh at me again, just as the door opened and Mr. Somerby and his mother came in.

They paused, as though surprised at his laughter and our apparent familiarity, and I saw a look come into Dyson's eyes that I was often to see when he looked at his brother — a sort of sharp wariness, which I soon learned to resent on Courtney's behalf. I could not understand anyone treating him with suspicion.

Dyson introduced me to his mother in his brusque manner. He had a touch of impatience when dealing with women and lived entirely in his man's world of management and business affairs.

Mrs. Somerby must have been in her sixties. She was very handsome, but painted and dressed to half her age.

Her eyes were like Courtney's and her hair dyed a chestnut colour. I dropped her a curtsy as she did not offer me her hand nor look at me but went straight to what was obviously her accustomed chair. It had a work box standing by it and she was always fiddling with embroidery which she never seemed to finish.

Mr. Somerby made all the elegant drawing-room furniture shrink to doll's house size, as though not a gilded chair in the whole room would support him.

It was difficult to believe they were related. I had heard it said that Sir Lockwood's sister had married beneath her. Her husband, Mr. Somerby, had been a manufacturer from the West Riding — he had lost all his money and been injured in a disastrous mill fire, dying while both her sons were still very young. Everyone said that Dyson was a real Somerby — certainly he was as different from his brother and mother as though he belonged to another race, like a big shire horse beside two elegant, highly strung thoroughbreds.

It appeared to me that he liked the situation as little as they did, but that he would doggedly do whatever he thought right. He did not regard me with mockery like Courtney, nor resentment, like his mother, but just accepted me — there I was and something had to be done about me. He was briefly and formally polite.

'Welcome to Sutherdyke, Isabel.'

'Thank you, sir.'

'You must call me Cousin Dyson, because you are my cousin. This is your Cousin Courtney. This is your Aunt Rose.'

His mother made a small, scornful noise which he ignored and went on speaking, stolidly determined to do his duty in the matter of this awkward cuckoo they had found in the nest.

'Mr. Shawcross, our lawyer, and I, have talked this

matter over. We have been granted legal guardianship of you until you are twenty-one. We have decided that you must go away to school. Mr. Shawcross has written to several establishments in the district to find somewhere suitable not too far away, but until then you will drive over to Miss Alfriston's every day for lessons. I'm afraid you will find it very dull here with no young people. We dine at six.'

'Isn't she too young to dine downstairs?' Mrs. Somerby spoke for the first time, and her high complaining voice made me think of Courtney's description of her 'wail of protest'. 'Cannot she have a meal in the old nursery?'

'What would you like to do, Isabel?' asked Dyson.

I lost heart. To dream of being a princess is one thing — to feel like a fisher lass from The Quay was another. I could have been pert with Mrs. Somerby and indifferent to Dyson but I passionately wanted Courtney's approval and notice. Everything was just too much. I wanted to creep away and hide.

To my astonishment, and perhaps to theirs, Courtney came and put his arm about my shoulders, saying with touching sweetness, 'The poor little brat is tired. Why don't you have dinner upstairs tonight, Isabel? Tomorrow my mother shall take you to buy some pretty new clothes, and then, when I'm home next time you will enjoy dining with us.'

I was a physically precocious thirteen, burgeoning with womanhood. I stood beneath the weight of that casually encircling arm, inwardly exploding with gratitude and delight. I could not trust myself to speak. Adoration must have shone in my eyes.

He knew of course. These magical charmers always do. I think it was from that moment he set out to put a spell on me as though I were a much older girl. Being kind to me when I was shy and awkward, helpful to me when I

43

made any crude mistakes of speech or manner. And — *touching me*. Casually, apparently disinterestedly, very subtly. A friendly arm about my shoulders as we walked together, my hand caught as I ran past, lifting me from my horse or down from a stile, or from the carriage so that the budding female within me became intoxicated with delight. While I was away from him I thought of nothing else, and when he was away in York with his regiment I starved with longing to see him again.

It was a condition I learned more about in the segregated intensity of a girls' boarding-school — the intense physical emotionalism of the very young. They called it 'being sweet' on someone . . . almost anyone from a senior girl to an actor whose picture was concealed in a textbook and mooned over in class, hidden beneath a pillow at night. At thirteen I breathed and lived for Courtney.

I do not think his mother noticed — I do not think that if he had attempted my seduction she would have noticed — or even cared. In her eyes he could do no wrong. But all the time during those weeks before he left for India and I went away to school I was conscious of Dyson watching and gravely disapproving. If I was chaperoned by my aunt, or by Janet, I guessed this was on Dyson's instructions. It became a fascinating game we played, part of the charm of it all, waiting for Courtney to arrive from York where he was stationed, and escaping their vigilance, laughing together, enthralled in our game of make-believe, indulgent on his part, deadly serious on mine, weaving plans and dreams of our future when he would have returned from India, and I would be grown up and rich.

'I will bring you back a slave with a jewel in her nose, and a white elephant with a gold howdah to ride on,' he once said.

But now, faced with the choice of dining in my rough

44

clothes or upstairs alone, I managed to say, 'Can I have my supper with Janet?'

'Who is Janet?' asked Mrs. Somerby.

'The little Bawtry girl, Mother, who works here,' said Dyson. 'Until recently Isabel thought of her as her sister.'

Mrs. Somerby cast her glance up at the painted stars in the ceiling as though invoking heavenly aid.

'Mother,' he said patiently. 'It is no fault of the child's. It is as difficult for her as for us.' He pulled the embroidered and tasselled bell-rope by the fireplace and Hawkins appeared so quickly that I thought he must have had his ear to the door.

'Will you ask Bawtry to show Miss Broadbent to her room and arrange for them to have dinner together in the old nursery. See a fire is lighted.'

'Yes, sir. Will you come this way, miss?'

As with Oldroyd — that 'miss' instead of his former patronising 'young woman' was a touch of balm. I was Miss Broadbent of Sutherdyke, after all, and there was nothing they could do about it. I put up my chin and followed him out into the hall with my nose in the air, and as the door closed behind us I heard Courtney's laughter.

Hawkins summoned a wide-eyed Janet from the kitchen, and when he repeated Dyson's instructions, 'Take Miss Broadbent up to her room' she dipped a curtsy! To *me*!

She took a lamp and led me demurely up the great stairway and into a big airy room with dark old furniture and rosy hangings and windows overlooking the lawns and rose-garden. As soon as the door shut behind us I flew into her arms and burst into tears of overstrain, loneliness and doubt, and she stroked my hair, and hugged me, and said, 'There, there, never fear, my little black love.'

But never for a minute did I consider running back to the cottage at Monkstonby Quay.

Janet and I dropped into our new roles of maid and mistress without any difficulty — she had always spoiled me and had looked after me since childhood — later I realised that it was her nature, in which there was not a particle of envy, that made this possible. She prompted me about dress and behaviour, and took a pride in my improvements. The first time I dined with the family downstairs she was glowing with triumph.

During the time before I was sent to school my life fluctuated between joy and boredom, according to whether Courtney was home or not. Sometimes when the time came for me to leave Miss Alfriston's it would be Courtney and not Oldroyd waiting in the trap and I flew out to join him on wings of love.

I was taught to ride and to handle reins on Dyson's instructions. He was firm about my having every advantage my position demanded. I had a daily lesson from Oldroyd, but whenever Courtney was home we went out together. I had a natural aptitude with horses and made a rapid progress, particularly when I realised Courtney admired my growing skill.

But the days when he was away at York, or off on a long week-end to London and the distractions of the West End, passed drearily. I moped about the big house, bored and lonely, longing for his return.

As the day for Courtney's departure approached my aunt became more and more distressed. She adored him and he was fond of her in an affectionate yet heartless way, knowing he could get his way with her over everything and nothing he did would incur her disapproval. He did not respect her — but I do not think he respected anyone.

She spoke about my position in my presence in a way that would have been insulting if it had not been so funny. Dyson could have left me where I was, she said. I would never have known, and therefore would have missed nothing. When I assured her that so far as I was concerned Courtney could have anything, she wailed that it was unfair that Dyson would not allow me to give away my fortune until I was of age. We both quite seriously thought it an injustice, and in my mind Dyson began to be a heartless, implacable guardian of the treasure, forbidding all delights. If in the make-believe game I had cast Courtney as the gallant Prince, now I cast Dyson as the Wicked Uncle, the Destroyer of Happiness, the Demon King. He could make us all so happy, and he would not, because my aunt told me he administered the whole estate, and to get him to advance the money for any little extra luxury was like getting blood out of a stone.

The little luxuries she spoke of were Courtney's debts. Expensive horses, expensive tailors, expensive wine and cigar merchants, large mess bills, a great deal of gambling. This, I was told, was the way a young gentleman was expected to live, and why not? I fervently agreed.

Janet said in her forthright way that she reckoned there were a lot of fast women too, but Mrs. Somerby did not mention this. I felt a pang of jealousy, but I did not really understand what Janet meant and she did not explain it in detail. But it all sounded very shocking, romantic and exciting — like the novels by Ouida and Marie Corelli that I found on my aunt's bookshelves, and if anything it added more to my handsome, mocking, dashing cousin's undoubted glamour.

Dyson was away a lot on business, always preoccupied, occasionally noticing me long enough to ask how I was doing, and barely listening to my reply, but for all that I think he knew all my movements. I was afraid of him, terrified when he summoned me to his office in the library to give me some instructions, although this was always for my own benefit. He insisted that his mother took time off from her social calls to send for patterns and a dressmaker to have new clothes for me, boots and shoes made at the bootmakers at Monkstonby and a fine new riding habit tailored to measure. I was equipped with sets of underwear, night wear, stockings, and a huge school trunk was ordered at the saddlers. My aunt did as she was bid, but I knew she resented every new expense on my behalf.

Gradually I became aware of the terrible disagreements about money that never ceased between the three of them. The unfinished sentences of accusation and reproach, left in the air when I entered a room. My aunt's complaining voice behind the closed door of the library, and the bitter quarrels between the brothers, Courtney's goading, gibing resentment flung endlessly at Dyson's impenetrable indifference.

My room was immediately above the library — I would lie in bed and hear their angry voices until far into the night.

I learned from my aunt that beside the settlements made on her and her sons, Dyson was paid a salary for managing the estate, and that she herself had inherited a small amount of money from her mother. Courtney had his pay and his settlement, and it was this which he and his mother thought would have been increased if my father had lived, and which Dyson, since my legitimacy had been acknowledged, insisted must be kept on the same level as it had been before Sir Lockwood's death. It was not, he said, their money, or his, to give.

Spurred into courage by my love for Courtney and my aunt's insistence, I found the courage to speak to Dyson. For the life of me I could not see why Courtney should not ship his polo ponies and his thoroughbred, Bantry Bay, out to India, together with a reasonable wine cellar and all the clothes, comforts, luxuries and furnishings which in my opinion he deserved.

Dyson listened to my faltering plea for five minutes, and then told me that Courtney was better off than most young officers, that his mother was indulgent and foolish, that I had better leave things I knew nothing about to those who did, and when I was twenty-one I could give Sutherdyke and everything else to the gypsies, so far as he was concerned, and would I not waste his time by talking a lot of blasted nonsense.

I crept away to report to my aunt feeling about two inches high and not in the least like Miss Broadbent of Sutherdyke, disliking Dyson as much as I loved his brother.

One morning I went downstairs in my riding habit quite early — it was Saturday, and there were no lessons with Miss Alfriston. I knew Courtney was home from York because I had heard raised voices late the night before and the slam of the doors that echoed through the great hall as they always did when Courtney worked himself up into a fury against his brother's clifflike indifference.

I found him fast asleep in an armchair in the morning room, a decanter of brandy and an empty glass on the table beside him. His boots were muddy, his beautiful pale fawn trousers torn about the knees as though he had been walking on the rough moorlands towards Dane's Dyke. I stood, hardly daring to breathe, wondering at the perfection of his red lips, the silken length of his closed eyelashes and the tumbled thickness of his bright hair. He half opened his eyes and grinned.

'Cousin Courtney,' I stammered, 'have you ever thought that if you married me when I am twenty-one then everything would belong to you?'

The long lashes lifted very slowly. He had extraordinary eyes — like the glass marbles I used to play with as a child. I do not mean they were protuberant, but the pupils were so small and the blue of the irises so transparent that the light seemed to strike through them as it does through glass or ice.

I felt a trembling excitement go through me. Before Bessy had put a stop to my playing with the rough lads on The Quay I had been grabbed and kissed and had neither liked nor disliked it especially — it had all been part of the puppy-vitality of our games. But the mere presence of my Cousin Courtney in the same room filled me with conflicting sensations. A terrible yearning — as though I would die if he touched me or would die if he did not.

'Yes, it had occurred to me — among other things. It is a pity you are only thirteen.' He smiled his sweet smile. 'I hear they have found you a school? Mama says they have settled on a place in Scarborough.'

'I don't want to go,' I said sullenly. 'I hate lessons. I don't want to be with a lot of girls.'

'You'd rather swim from the coves and beat the boys about the head when they spy on you without your petticoats?'

I went scarlet. 'Who told you . . .' and stopped, biting my lips, his laughter telling me I had given myself away.

'Company I keep.'

Janet had told me that when he was bored or angry, had quarrelled with his brother or wanted to plague his mother he would go off alone to The Crown at Norhead Green, where the poachers and gambling men made much of him, and I thought he must have been there that night and some man from the town had talked about me.

'Don't be angry, little cousin,' he said, sweet again. 'I like bold girls. I hate milk-and-water misses. You have just proposed to me and I have decided to accept. Consider yourself engaged to marry me in six years' time. Now, give me a few minutes to change and we will take a ride together.'

He pulled himself up out of the chair and I threw my arms round him. He disengaged himself laughingly. I raced out to the stables while he went to change. I was not going to ride the fat white pony which drew the gig — not with Courtney by my side on his magnificent Bantry. I told Oldroyd to saddle me the mare, and when I told him that Courtney was coming with me and when he agreed I sighed with relief.

The bright little mare snickered and danced a bit when she was led out, but when I mounted she stood quietly enough and I sat, proud as a peacock when Courtney came out, breeched and booted, and swung up on the big red-coated hunter.

'Now, sir,' warned Oldroyd, 'don't let Miss do anything daft like. No jumps. We're coming on a fair treat but we're not a rider yet.'

'Aren't we?' said Courtney coolly. 'Shall I take you on a leading rein, Isabel?' I glared at them both and took Ladybird out of the stable-yard in style, my nose in the air.

We went out towards Norhead, riding over the open moorland, right to the end of the headland. We did not talk because the wind caught our voices and tossed them up into the clear air. We crossed Dane's Dyke by a bridged drain, and cantered along the short sheep-cropped grass until we reached the cliff's edge, and there reined in, looking down the crumbling chalk slope to the waves crashing on the boulders below.

Bantry stood steadily but the little mare did not like it. She stamped and sidled, trying to get away from the cliff-edge, so I reined her in and turned not afraid myself, and found Courtney was looking at me with those transparent eyes as he had looked when I had naïvely suggested he should marry me. I had an intense vision of the possible. He had only to bring his riding crop down across the little mare's haunches to send her and me sliding and scrambling to our deaths. I felt myself go white.

'Why do you look like that?' he exclaimed.

I told him, and he too changed colour.

'*Isabel*! How could you think such a thing?'

'I don't know ... it came to me. You would have nothing to fret over then — neither you nor your mother.'

'If you believe it — why don't you ride away?'

I was still under the spell, the premonition, whatever it was ... not in a glass darkly, but brilliantly clear like a white light inside my brain.

'I know you couldn't bring yourself to do anything to hurt me however much you might want to. Others, maybe, but never me.'

'You are a witch,' he said, 'a little witch. And you are wrong. I was only thinking that I have been up all night and if I don't get some sleep I shall fall off my horse.'

He caught my bridle and drew me away from the edge and as we cantered back, my vision and the sense of white brilliant light left me, but I felt tired with a drained sense of helplessness.

In the stable-yard he lifted me down, with some concern for I was still pale, and put his arm about me as we went into the hall, holding me against him. As I looked up, he kissed me and I thought I would faint.

His lips only just brushed mine — but I shook against him with uncontrollable emotion. I was exposed and at his mercy, too young and inexperienced, too chaotic to know what was happening to me.

'Women,' he said, 'are all the same. Whatever their age.'

I stared uncomprehendingly, and he laughed.

'Poor little brat,' he said. 'Aren't you going to kiss me

too? Cousins kiss, and engaged couples. We are both, after all.'

Whether I would have returned his kiss I do not know for there was the sound of a door opening somewhere within the house; his arm fell away from me and with one wild, imploring look, I fled away from him to my room.

Before dinner Hawkins came to say that Mr. Somerby would like to see me in the library before dinner.

Dyson was sitting at his desk, waiting for me. He motioned me to a chair and said, 'You are thirteen, Isabel?'

'Yes.'

'You look older. You look sixteen.'

I was delighted to hear this, but said nothing.

'My mother has been over to Scarborough to see Mrs. Thorncliffe's Academy for young ladies. She tells me it is very suitable. Most of the local young ladies are boarders there. Mrs. Thorncliffe can take you.'

'When?' I said aghast. Courtney had only three more weeks before he sailed.

'At once,' said Dyson. 'It is Friday — you can be ready to go on Monday.'

'Can't I stay until Courtney goes?'

'No.'

'Why not?'

He looked at me silently and I felt myself going hot under his dispassionate gaze.

'Isabel,' he said, 'young lasses are like young bitches or young mares — you have to watch them all the time when their blood begins to stir. I haven't the time nor my mother the inclination to play chaperon to you, but you are my responsibility. You'll be far better off at school until your Cousin Courtney has left and you've had a chance to learn a bit of sense.'

If I had nearly fainted from emotion earlier, I nearly exploded with fury at this.

'I'm not one of your ewes out on the wolds, damn you!'
I shouted, 'and I'm going to marry Courtney when I'm
old enough. When he's back from India. I shall wait for
him and I shan't look at another chap, no, not if he was a
bloody prince!'

His straight brows drew together and he rubbed his
upper lip with the thumbnails of his folded hands. He had
a habit of doing this when he talked to me, hiding his
mouth, so that I never knew whether he was angry or
laughing at me, for his grey eyes never changed their
expression.

'Well, then, you'll need to know a great deal more of
life than how to ride a horse and curse like a fishwife.
You're not the only heiress in the world. Think of all the
beautiful, rich young women Courtney might meet in the
next few years. Don't fancy your chances too highly, my
lass.'

This blunt statement brought me back to reality and
my immediate reaction was to plunge into despair.

'I'll never learn,' I cried. 'Happen you'd better give
him all the money and let me go back to Aunt Bessy on
The Quay.'

'Aye, and happen I will,' he said with such gravity that
at first I did not see he was quietly mocking me, 'if tha
doesn't do as I tell thee. Get off upstairs now, and tell
Bawtry to pack your things, and let's have no more nonsense.' I started to the door, and he called me back.
'Isabel, my mother has complained that you go over to
Monkstonby each week to see Mrs. Bawtry.'

'I always shall,' I glowered.

'I'm glad you do. I do not share my mother's view of
this. It is right that you should continue to know someone
who has been so kind to you.'

I looked at him uncomprehendingly, only interested in
Courtney, my longing to please him and my despair at

being sent away. That I had somehow pleased Dyson by continuing to visit Bessy meant nothing to me at all.

I went sullenly upstairs, told Janet to pack my things, and spent the time before dinner putting on a new white-dotted muslin with a pink under-dress, and trying my hair in different ways, finally tying it with a big rose-coloured bow. My efforts were wasted because Courtney had left by the evening train for London. My aunt was tearful about this, grudging every minute of his time away from her, and Dyson was silent and preoccupied.

Bereft and bemused I pretended to eat, indulging in those intense romantic daydreams that only adolescents know. Adults forget these dreams and the joy and despair that accompany them.

When I realised that I would not see Courtney before he went away I felt as though I had died and I blamed Dyson for my unhappiness. He did not care for anything but the money. I was sure he had seen Courtney and me together in the hall and so was sending me away. That, under the circumstances, dealing with a physically pre-cocious, passionate girl of thirteen years, his decision had been correct, never entered my head. He had torn me from my idol and I hated him.

I remember gripping my hands beneath the carriage rug as I was driven to the station on Monday, and praying that Courtney would appear miraculously to bid me farewell at the station. But he did not, and my aunt accompanied me to Scarborough and delivered me into Mrs. Thorncliffe's care.

I stayed at school for five years and six months, only returning to Sutherdyke for the holidays. When I returned at Christmas Courtney was already in Calcutta. I learned a lot of things at school, useful lessons, fashionable accomplishments, lost my Quayside accent and made many girl friends among the local families. At first I wrote secret, passionate letters to Courtney in India and bribed one of the school maids to post them. He never replied and in my fifteenth year I became self-conscious and stopped writing to him. In my eighteenth year, during my final term at Mrs. Thorncliffe's in Scarborough, I heard that my aunt had had a letter from India telling her that he was resigning his commission, through ill-health, he said, and was coming home. All the old longing and love welled up within me again as the term drew to an end. I had longed to leave school, to be grown up, and now, better than all this, Courtney was returning and I prayed that he would be returning to me.

CHAPTER THREE

I was in my eighteenth year, tall, supple, slender and as beautiful, or so people said, as my mother had been. I was delighted to be free and had stayed on at school so long only because, so far as I could see, Dyson did not quite know what to do with me. My aunt was getting older, and he had no inclination to escort a debutante around in local society.

He was thirty now, unchanged, watching my affairs and progress with meticulous attention to his duty. If he was pleased with me he said so briefly. If he was angry at any neglect on my part I received a sharp reprimand which I feared far more than I had William Bawtry's heavy hand in childhood. If his bright, wary, observant eyes found me attractive he did not say so. Plenty of other men did, though, and I was soon being talked of as a local catch and the belle of the county.

I had a curious relationship with Dyson, for although he considered me a child and a burden, he was also determined that I should have some grasp of my affairs and my future position as owner of Sutherdyke.

During the school holidays he would occasionally take me to Leeds or Hull with him on business trips. I thought I should find it a great bore, but it was fascinating. Under Dyson's management my capital had been invested in many things besides land and property; mining, finance, the wool trade, and flour milling. I would sit demurely silent in the mahogany-panelled offices while the men talked. Sometimes I would take lunch with them in a hotel dining-room. No one paid me more than a fleeting attention and the talk was all of business. My aunt considered it all very improper and unnecessary and my interest most unladylike.

I was astounded by this side of Dyson. Nothing dry-as-dust here. He seemed to dominate this world of business-men. He was highly respected among them and was a little feared. Coming back to Monkstonby on the train we would talk about the affairs of the estate and I enjoyed it as much as he.

'You're no fool, Isabel,' was the greatest compliment I ever had from him, who expected all women to be foolish and unreliable.

Dyson was brilliant with men, management, money and business. Feelings and affections he did not seem to understand. His mother said he was dead to what she considered the finer side of life. He did not appear to have an ounce of romance in his whole nature. He enjoyed making money, not for the money itself, for most of what he made belonged to me, but because of his ability to manipulate men and affairs. He lived comfortably and he saw that I had everything warranted by my position. But he had no interest in luxury for its own sake, and the people he understood best were the people who worked for him who seemed to give him loyalty and a grudging affection.

But all this was forgotten and disregarded now that I knew that at long last Courtney was coming home. My aunt and I talked of nothing else. I was filled with a passionate longing to see him again and the memory of his bright, boyish good-looks filled my mind. I could not imagine myself loving any other man. Aunt Rose and I spent our days in excited anticipation of his homecoming. Courtney's room must be redecorated and prepared. The wine cellar must be checked and his favourite vintages ordered. The horses must be ready — Bantry, now a steady ten-year-old and a fine hunter, must be kept in trim for him. We wondered about his health, how ill he really had been. We told ourselves that a short while in the good East Riding air would soon make him well again. He was twenty-six now — nearly twenty-seven, but we could only visualise the beautiful boy of twenty who had gone so reluctantly away to India nearly six long years ago.

Dyson listened to us dourly, occasionally dropping an ironical or restraining comment. I lost all interest in the business of the estate, apart from my plans for Courtney's comfort, so he did not ask me to accompany him on his business trips that summer. But when one day he called me into the library and said that he thought it would be a good idea if I went to London for six months with my friend May Lister and her mother to have a taste of fashionable life, I was horrified. Leave Sutherdyke just when Courtney was coming home? It was unthinkable!

Dyson said he had spoken to Mr. Lister about it. Mr. Lister was a business friend and owned a large estate in the neighbourhood, Fieldhouse Grange. May had been very excited at the idea of a London season, but this was the first mention of my sharing it with her.

During the term, before Courtney's letter had arrived, I would have been delighted at the idea, but now when we knew he was coming, though not exactly when, I could not bear it. I burst into a storm of protest, most of it quite illogical, throwing my trumped-up reasons at Dyson like a child throwing pebbles at a rock face. He sat at his desk listening silently, solid and, I feared, unyielding, for I knew nothing would budge him if he had made up his mind.

My aunt had once shown me a faded photograph of

herself and her two boys, Courtney sprawling in golden indolence on her knee, Dyson, a farmer's-lad sort of a child with a forthright stare and a lot of freckles. She had sighed, 'A perfect little Somerby. Look at him — not an ounce of grace or sweetness, not like the Broadbents at all.'

So I went on with my tirade until I could think of nothing else and my voice petered out, while he hid his mouth behind his folded hands and watched me. Then he said briskly, 'Right! Through all the last holidays you were saying there's little to do here but ride, hunt and drive over to Fieldhouse to gossip with May. Now suddenly, nothing will induce you to go away. Give me the real reason for this change of heart.'

'Courtney is coming home.'

'He has not even sailed yet.'

'But he will, at any time. I cannot be away for six months. I must be here when he returns. I must, I must! I believe you just want me to go away because he is coming.'

For a moment he did not speak.

'Aye,' he said, 'I thought that was what you thought.'

I managed to control my temper. I had learned over the years that it cut no ice with Dyson. I had not met many men — only the fathers and brothers of my school friends, but I had learned that it was easier to get one's own way with charm and persuasion than by sulking. For the first time in my life I tried these tactics with Dyson. Why not? I knew I would get nowhere by fighting him. I knew I had a siren's legacy in my blood from my mother. Why not keep my temper and see how he would react to a sweet docility?

I stopped ranting and went round the desk and sat on a low stool at his feet, linking my hands over his knee, my chin upon my hands. Although I still wore my hair down, I was a young woman now, tall and slender, with all my

60

mother's tense, dark beauty. As I looked up his face might have been carved in stone.

'Cousin Dyson,' I said. 'Please don't send me away. I have been away for eight months of every year since I came to live here. And you cannot expect me *not* to be excited when Courtney is coming home. I know it was all silliness . . . I mean that talk about being engaged. I was only a baby. But I am fond of him, and we did have fun.'

He put out a long finger and lifted the hair back from my forehead and I felt my skin shiver unexpectedly, like my mare Ladybird, when I gentled her. I could not remember that he had ever touched me before.

'Fun?' he said. 'What does that word mean?'

I supposed he had never had any — since he had left school he had always been looking after other people's affairs.

'If you don't know how to enjoy yourself it's not fair to stop other people doing so. It's not their fault if you prefer to work and worry and order us all about.'

I knew that had struck home and felt a little scared. His massive anger was rarely roused, but it could be overwhelming.

'You have known nothing but a girl's boarding-school and the small circle of people round Sutherdyke. You are setting your heart on a child's dream. If I need to buy anything do I choose the first thing I see? No. I take my time. I look around. I make sure I get the best available. I think you should look around.'

'But people aren't things,' I stormed, forgetting my intention of charming him. 'You think of everything and everyone as though it's a matter of business.'

He leaned back smiling grimly, and I knew he had seen through me.

'That's more like it,' he said. 'Haven't I had reason to think so? And you can thank me for it. You wouldn't have much to tempt Courtney or any other young scamp if it had not been for me.'

'People have feelings — I won't have a husband valued and bought as though he were a load of hay!'

'It's no use flashing your big black eyes and stamping your feet at me. And it's no use playing your kitten tricks either. I am telling you not to expect everything to be the same when Courtney returns. Six years have passed.'

He was voicing my secret fears.

'You mean — he may have forgotten me?'

'It is possible.'

I would not think of such a possibility. I tried a new tack. 'My aunt wants me with her. As you know, Courtney has been ill, that is why he has given up the army.'

'So he says.'

'He has had continuous fever. He may need caring for. My aunt wants me to stay.'

'My mother only wants what she thinks is best for him. She thinks her brother's money, which you will inherit when you are twenty-one, would be very good for him. She even thinks he has a right to it.' I detected a real bitterness in his voice. 'As she thinks he has a right to everything.'

The tears came to my eyes.

'You make everyone sound horrible. If Aunt Rose loves him more than you, you cannot blame her — he is always nice to her. He was kind to me when I first came when I was little and shy, and unhappy. Why should I not like him?'

'Have I not been kind to you?'

'You have done what you thought was right — that's all.'

There was a long silence and the domed brass clock on the mantelpiece struck the hour. I looked up at him with a feeling of dismay. I had meant to hurt him and for the first time I had. I had always thought him invulnerable. I felt very young and inadequate. I wished I had held my spiteful tongue. But my determination not to leave Sutherdyke this summer remained unshakable.

The library always smelled of leather bindings and dust because there were so many deed-boxes and filed papers that the servants could never clean it as meticulously as they did the rest of the house. Dry-as-dust Dyson, I thought. I wondered if he was going to dismiss me without another word and the silence lengthened uncomfortably.

A log fell from the fire into the hearth and the long-legged springer bitch who was his constant companion leaped for safety. He put the log back, and patted her reassuringly.

'There now, Sally . . . there, lass . . .'

'You are more understanding with your dog than you are with your mother or brother, *or* me,' I cried.

He straightened up and his eyes were bright with anger.

'Right,' he said, 'we'll let it drop. I'll ask the Listers to wait until the summer is over and we will think about it again.'

Relief flooded over me, shone in my eyes and smile. He went back to his desk, and drew his papers before him. 'Now get off and let me work — and don't play the fool with Courtney when he comes back. He isn't a boy and you are no longer a child.'

I had been reprieved. I did not care what he thought. I raced through to the blue drawing-room where my Aunt Rose sat working at her everlasting embroidery and burst out with the news of my narrow escape from banishment.

She listened, her habitual expression of refined complaint brightening to anger.

Aunt Rose tolerated me and I had learned a great deal from her of the surface values of manners, conventions and clothes. I think she was a little proud of the result but

63

there was no affection between us — no warm embrace or kiss such as I had on my weekly visits to Bessy Bawtry in her cottage by the Quayside. I felt that all her love was given to Courtney, and she had none to spare for anyone else.

He was our great mutual interest. We waited for his infrequent letters and she read me extracts from them. At first he had seemed to like army life in India. There was polo, the horse-racing, the officers' mess, the club, the parties and balls. But during the last years a malaise seemed to have fallen over him. He seemed to see all the ugliness, none of the beauty, he hated the climate and more particularly the people, and longed to return home. Ill health, my aunt said, had changed him. She had written telling him not to hesitate to resign his commission and come back to Sutherdyke.

I had drawn a small chair up near her, and began to thread her silks. I often did this for her. She had tried to teach me to embroider but I found it boring. I was a physical creature, loving to use my body to the full, riding, driving, walking — swimming from the Norhead coves but now in a discreet costume and with Janet in watchful attendance. I loved dancing best of all, my talent was inborn, rhythmic and theatrical, reminding everyone of my mother, a sensation in the refined classes at Mrs. Thorncliffe's Academy.

We sat in silence for a while — a fire flickered in the hearth although it was a warm May evening. There was a glass screen to protect us from its heat. My aunt was full of these rather delicate, old-fashioned affectations.

'Dyson hates Courtney,' she said, so unexpectedly that I stared.

'Oh no,' I protested. 'It is only his way.'

'No. He hates his brother. He always has. I suppose I am to blame — I could never love Dyson as a boy. He was

64

so alien to me — the great creature! No atom of grace — his father's boy. His father loved him — when he died it was the only time I have seen Dyson cry. When Courtney was born he was always jealous of him. I had to protect Courtney from his spite.'

She looked up at the portrait of my mother above the hearth. The one with the background of blue Spanish tiles. She never spoke my mother's name. 'That dancer,' she sometimes said, as she might have said. 'That whore,' for she had an eighteenth century frankness of speech at times.

'When *she* died, Sir Lockwood told me to come to live at Sutherdyke and bring my boys, and so I did. What else could I do? I was a widow. I had only the money my mother had left me. Dyson worked so hard to please Sir Lockwood but, of course, my brother despised him, as he did all the Somerby family. He never forgave me for marrying a Somerby. But he was fond of Courtney, who amused him. He found him charming, and in his sober moments made a great deal of him. This made the breach between my sons worse. Dyson could never please my brother, while Courtney always did, without trying. But now Dyson has come into his own. Now he rules us all.'

I carefully inserted the threaded needles into the red satin cushion, shading them from crimson to palest pink, night blue to azure, bright yellow to pale cream, so that my aunt could take them like colours from a palette. I found myself rather sorry for the big, freckled, unloved boy trying so hard to repay his uncle for his generosity, and getting no thanks for it.

'Did you not wonder why Dyson should want to send you away?'

I bent over my task so she should not see the colour in my cheeks.

'Oh well,' I said, as casually as I was able, 'I was rather a goose over Courtney. I expect Dyson thinks I've no more sense than I had at thirteen.'

'Oh, no.' She put her embroidery frame down on her knee. It held a piece of cream satin on which she was working a wreath of roses, morning glory and hovering butterflies — to what purpose I did not know. She pressed her useless and exquisite work with her small white hand, looking down on it with a strange complacency. The bearer of mysteries. 'Ah, no, Isabel, that's not it at all. He wants you and your fortune for himself.'

'*Dyson?*' I said incredulously. 'I'm simply a nuisance to him.'

There was a wall mirror framed in blue Venetian glass on the opposite wall. She rose, took my hand and led me to it, showed me my slim, tall, dark reflection.

'You are a beautiful girl — Dyson is not so indifferent as he appears to be. He may have no delicacy but he has strong passions like his father.' There was distaste in her voice. 'But his real passion is to prevent any understanding between you and Courtney and to make his own position at Sutherdyke secure. Since my brother's first stroke everything has been in Dyson's hands. Do you think he wishes to relinquish it? That is why he wants to prevent you meeting his brother again, now, when you are really old enough to fall in love.'

She collected her reticule, her fan and lorgnettes, and went from the room. I stood alone; the picture of my mother above the hearth looked down at me, the long hair slipping over her bare shoulders, her soft, tempting mouth smiling at my astonishment, as though it amused her to find me discovering that beauty is a mixed blessing after all.

Courtney's departure seemed continually delayed — it was more difficult than he had anticipated to settle everything up and get away, and it was the end of July when we received a definite sailing date.

At last we could relax a little. While it had been indefinite we had imagined him walking in on us at any time. It was, as Aunt Rose said, exactly the sort of trick that would amuse him. But now we knew he could not land in England before September we decided to go to Harrogate for two weeks for a change and to do some shopping. We stayed at a hotel and Aunt Rose took the waters and we met and gossiped with friends. I went to a few dances and we bought some pretty clothes. The most memorable thing about that fortnight was that I put my hair up, and at once felt quite old and *distinguée*.

The first evening at dinner after our return I wore a trailing low-cut gown and a rose fastened into my high-dressed hair. Dyson came in and stopped, staring at me across the room as though he had never seen me before.

I preened a little, watching him, then he said that I looked very grand, and immediately spoiled it by adding that however I did my hair, up or down, it did not signify that I had any more sense in my head.

I decided that his mother must be mad to suggest that he was interested in me. In the Broadbent money perhaps — Dry-as-Dust-Dyson, unpleasant, harsh, deflating Dyson — blunt as a wold farmer with his rough North Country manner.

There was a heat-wave that summer so that it was too hot to ride, or play croquet or walk until the evening cooled the air. It was a wonderful harvest — the wolds ochre with grain as far as the eye could see. I visited my friends and went on summer outings, picnic parties, and garden parties and visited Scarborough. I wore my pretty new clothes and flirted with deliberate coquetry and encouraging effect on the young men of my acquaintance. But I kept an armour over my bespoke heart and waited, and waited and *waited* for the time when Courtney would return.

Then one hot day an incident happened, brief and fierce like a summer storm. May Lister, my best friend, drew me aside at the vicarage garden party, pink-faced and potent with mystery and said, 'I hear your cousin Courtney is returning from India?'

'He's already on his way,' I said. 'Oh May, I'm longing to see him again.'

'I feel I should tell you, Isabel, that I was at a regimental ball at York while you were in Harrogate with Mrs. Somerby, and I heard some bad things about him.'

My temper flared defensively. I would hear nothing against Courtney.

'I don't want to hear your horrid gossip.'

'Oh, very well.'

She turned away, but I caught her sleeve — I really did want to know.

'You might as well tell me now.'

'There was an officer who had been in India and I danced with him. He said that Lieutenant Somerby had been involved in scandalous behaviour and his colonel had *asked* him to resign his commission.'

'Courtney is a man and not one of your namby-pamby curates,' I said furiously. May always attracted curates. Her snubby, blonde prettiness seemed to have a fatal attraction for them.

'I'm only warning you,' she said crossly. 'If you're stupid enough to be moony over a rake, I can't help it. It's just that this man said Courtney was thrown out.'

'And what was this great scandal?' I asked.

'Well, of course he wouldn't tell me, but he told Mother, and I got a little out of her. It was something about a woman — a native woman.'

For a moment I was as shocked as May. But Courtney

was not here to defend himself, and I was determined not to believe her.

'There's no need to glare like that. I only told you for your own good.'

'You told me because you are a mischief-maker. Courtney is Courtney — he is streets better than any man in this county. You and your gossiping mother had better be careful what you say.'

May tossed her rose-trimmed bonnet and walked away, and at once I ran after her, putting my arm through hers.

'May, I'm sorry. I don't mean to be a beast, but I know Courtney and you don't, and if you did you would not believe anything bad about him. But I would hate Aunt Rose to hear this, because it would distress her so.'

Mollified, May promised not to gossip, and I knew she would keep her word. Her pretty fair face cleared, and she kissed me, and said, 'But do take care, Bella. You're so impulsive!'

But what she had said stayed in my mind all afternoon. I did not believe it, and I knew my aunt would not believe it either. Courtney might do something dashing, reckless, wild or foolish I knew, but nothing scandalous. I did not want Dyson to hear this story. He was angry enough about Courtney giving up his army career and coming home, and such a rumour would be another weapon against the attractive brother whom he disliked so much.

September came and they brought the harvest home, and the great silver moon made a glittering path across the sea. It rained, cleared, and left the county cold and autumnal, so we could ride to the meets again, and plan our winter entertainments. The most exciting for me was my nineteenth birthday, when I had been promised a ball at Sutherdyke.

Then at last we read that the SS *Peshawar* had docked at Southampton. All day and the next three days we waited for the letter or telegram to announce Courtney's arrival. It did not come.

My aunt was in such a state of hysterical apprehension that Dyson almost gave in to her demands to be taken instantly to London and thence to Southampton to make first-hand inquiries, and then there came a letter from London, so casual, that to me it was almost like a slap in the face. We had been waiting for so long to see him. I felt hurt and was bitterly sorry for my aunt.

Courtney said he had shipped his polo ponies back to England, and he was going to sell them at Tattersalls' while he was in London — or take any good, private offer. He had to stay to see prospective buyers and attend to the sale. He was enjoying being in London again. His heavy luggage would soon arrive and he hoped to be in Sutherdyke before long — but on no account was his mother to come to London as he was very busy and might have to go out to Newmarket. He was sorry, but he had heavy expenses and needed the money from the sale of his string. With this we had to be content. Aunt Rose became more tense and I was wild with impatience and indignation. I longed to see him but began to realise he was not equally anxious to see me. Perhaps Dyson was right and he had forgotten me.

We settled down again to the interminable waiting. My aunt was just as lovingly anxious, just as ready to make excuses, but I was feeling a certain amount of resentment.

One evening, when she shook her head unhappily, and said, 'No news again. When will he come?' I replied sharply. 'He'll come when he wants to, no doubt. And there is other news. Have you heard that Ivy Lodge has a new tenant? Is it true, Dyson?'

Ivy Lodge was the nearest house to Sutherdyke apart from the cottages in the village. It was not very large. An isolated villa, it was, as its name implied, ivy-clad and stood at the end of a winding avenue of dark hollies and firs, a gloomy-looking place. It had been empty for over a year. I had noticed as I rode home that evening, that there were some lights about the house, and smoke coming from the chimneys.

'Yes,' Dyson said, 'a Mrs. McAllister has taken it. It has been arranged through a London agent. She is a widow and has been living abroad. There is a small boy, I believe.'

'Is she a suitable tenant for Broadbent property?' I asked.

If he realised my mockery he gave no hint of it — that was not Dyson's way.

'I am not sure at all. It is a sub-letting and does not concern me.'

'Well, now, I should have thought you would have investigated even that. Have you seen this lady?' I was not interested in the widowed Mrs. McAllister, or Ivy Lodge. But I was determined for one evening not to talk about Courtney.

'I have not,' said Dyson. 'As I have said it is not my responsibility.' He smiled, as though offering me a truce. His rare smile was the only touch of Broadbent about him. 'And since you have decided that we are going to have one evening without bewailing Courtney's absence and wondering when he will condescend to return home, let us have some music. Come into the drawing-room and play for us.'

The colour flooded my cheeks, he had so accurately guessed my thoughts. But I went with them into the drawing-room and played and sang for them and did not once mention Courtney. The following morning my aunt received a telegram to say he would arrive the following day. She burst into tears of relief.

I did not suggest that I should accompany her to the

station. While I waited for them to return I changed my dress three times, until even my stolid Janet became impatient. I fussed about my hair and tried it half a dozen ways, and then when I heard the sound of carriage wheels I felt cold and sick with excitement, and sat in my room not daring to go down until my aunt sent for me.

'Oh, Janet,' I said, terrified I was going to burst into tears after all and make myself look ugly, 'Supposing he doesn't like me?'

'Nay, he will that. Look at thyself in t'glass, love.'

I looked doubtfully at my reflection, at the high-piled black hair, the big, dark eyes and thought of all the beautiful girls Courtney must have met since I saw him last. Was there someone in India whom he had not mentioned? Had he met anyone in London during the past weeks? Was that why he had lingered there?

I went downstairs and timidly opened the door of the blue drawing-room, remembering the first time I had spoken to him, a child of thirteen and he had seemed to be the most glorious young man in all the world.

He was standing in his old place, behind his mother's chair. He looked at me above her head with an expression of disbelief, as though he was rejecting what he saw. As though he had hoped I would be different, and then he said, almost inaudibly, 'But it can't be . . .'

'Indeed it is Isabel,' said his mother indulgently. 'For shame, darling — you're embarrassing the poor child.'

Then he came to life, crossed the room and took my hands.

'My little cousin Isabel!'

'I warned you that she was very pretty.'

'Pretty! She is beautiful.'

'It is like the old days when you both used to talk about me as though I was not there,' I said. 'I don't like it. Will you still call me a brat?'

'Did I do that?' He laughed, recovered something of his old lightness and gaiety. 'What a young cad I must have been! Did you dislike me very much?'

We were pretending to flirt, the words meaning nothing, our eyes feverishly rediscovering each other.

'You know how she adored you,' said my aunt.

'I have done a great deal of growing up since then,' I said.

He had changed. There was a burned-out, exciting look about him, the imp in the boy had become a seductive devil in the man. The purity of his young beauty had gone, but he was very handsome. There were signs of his illness. He was thin and there was a yellowing tinge in his fair skin — even in the whites of the transparent azure eyes.

I do not know how well he remembered me or what sort of girl he had expected to see, but as I sat there listening to them talk I was aware that his glance returned continuously, almost helplessly to me, and it gave me a new sense of power, exhilarating but confused, like drinking champagne.

We waited for Dyson, who was delayed, and Courtney told us about India and how he hated everything about it. The limited society of the army stations, the social conventions of the army community, 'Mrs. Lieutenant salaaming to Mrs. Captain, and so on up the hierarchy until you come to Mrs. Viceroy, then to the dear Queen — and then, presumably, to God, who makes it awkward by not being married — at least not officially.'

'You really are a naughty boy,' said my aunt, smiling.

'It's not funny at all.' I recognised the old shift of mood from gaiety to despair and he seemed closer to me. 'It eats your sanity away. The beggars and the flies, the smell of burning dung and marigolds. The bazaars where anything or anybody can be bought.'

She stared at him uncomprehendingly. He pulled the bell cord and when Hawkins came told him to bring the whisky decanter and, as he poured himself a drink, said, 'This is another insidious Indian habit. The chota-peg. The little drink. When the heat and the boredom close down on you you clap your hands and a brown genie appears and pours you one, and a second, and a third until you finish up with a piece of leather instead of a liver.'

'My dear boy,' said my aunt fondly, 'I hope you haven't acquired any such bad habits.'

He looked at her sombrely for a moment, then laughed, drank off his glass, and refilled it.

'I have acquired no virtues, Mama, nor anything I wanted. Everything I wanted was here at Sutherdyke.'

He looked at me with that strange look, and I felt my cheeks flush and my heart-beats quicken. I asked him some trivial question about India, trying to conceal my confusion, and then he smiled understandingly, with all the old sweetness, and it was as though he had touched me.

At last, just as the dinner gong went, Dyson came in. The two brothers stood for a moment, looking at each other silently for a moment, and then Dyson put out his hand, and Courtney took it with a wry smile.

'Well, Dyson, you're the only person here from whom I don't expect a whole-hearted welcome.'

The contrast between the brothers was extraordinary — Dyson like a great oak tree beside Courtney's slender grace. I saw Courtney's mocking wince as Dyson released his hand.

'Still as heavy-handed,' he said, and Dyson turned him towards one of the lamps saying, kindly enough, 'Let's have a look at you, lad. You're thin — and a bit jaundiced. What have you been doing to yourself?'

Courtney jerked angrily away. 'I was devilish sick.'

'Well, Mother and Isabel will enjoy cosseting you — and Isabel has kept Bantry in fine fettle for you to ride again.'

Courtney gave him a long, hard look. 'No questions about my resignation? No confidential talk in the library?'

'We will have to talk about your future of course.' There was an edge in Dyson's voice. 'But get well first. There is plenty of time.'

The second gong sounded. My aunt took Courtney's arm, and he immediately turned and offered me his other, so the three of us went in together, leaving Dyson to follow behind, and I knew that nothing had really changed. There were two camps in the house bitterly oppressed, and always would be when the two brothers were there together.

Courtney joined us in the drawing-room immediately after dinner, while Dyson excused himself, saying he had to deal with the post that had come during the day. My aunt made a fuss about not having her châtelaine with her thimble and scissors, and insisted on going to fetch them herself.

'Alone at last! Mama really could not have made it more obvious — so let us take advantage of it. How do you find me, Isabel? Changed?'

'Changed,' I echoed.

'Older?'

'Of course.'

'Dissipated?'

'Yes.'

'You don't like what you see?'

'I didn't say that.' I was evasive, trying to sound light. 'But I shall have plenty of time to discover all about you ... What do you think of me?'

'Tonight when you came through that door I understood

75

Sir Lockwood's passion for your mother,' he said. 'You are all her portraits — but alive. I have been told she was a woman to drive men mad and so are you.'

I had not expected this. He must have realised I was a little afraid for he said with a sudden, passionate sincerity, 'Do you remember once you said you knew that whatever happened I could never hurt you? Tonight I realise what that means. Whatever I have been, whatever I am now, whatever I intended, I could never hurt you.'

'Intended?'

'Intended to do with my life.' He kissed me full on the lips quite calmly and gently. 'But for both our sakes, Isabel, don't tempt me too far. I do not find it easy to be a good man.'

The child he had left would have thrown her arms about him but the girl I had become drew back uncertainly.

'But don't be afraid — never of me.'

'What is there to be afraid of?'

He searched my face intently, then turned away, saying abruptly, 'Go and help Mama find whatever it is she pretends she has lost, or she will be upstairs for the whole evening.'

Out of his sight I raced upstairs for the shelter of my own room. I opened the door on to surprising darkness and found Janet standing by the window looking down into the rose-garden below. When I spoke to her she started and I went to her side.

'What are you doing in the dark, Janet? What can you see outside?'

I looked out but could only see the outline of the yew hedges and faintly the stone cupid on the fountain. Nothing else.

'I think I saw the ghost, Miss Isabel. Thy mother . . . she walks there, they say.'

'You saw *what*?'

'I couldn't say rightly now, but something white, ower there, in t'garden...'

'Something or someone?'

'Someone — I opened the window and it went away towards the orchard.'

'Oh, Janet, it was one of the maids running off to meet her sweetheart.' I felt quite cross. It was so unlike Janet. 'For goodness' sake light the lamps and draw the curtains and stop seeing ghosts.'

But when she set the lampglass back and turned up the flame, I could see that her square, sensible face was deadly white and her hands were trembling.

'Why, Janet, you *are* upset. Did you *really* see something?'

'They say Sir Lockwood had a daybed put here for her the summer she died, and he sat with her all day, willing her to live, or so Mrs. Oldroyd told me, and she trying to escape in the only way she knew. By dying. They say he would have bought her back from the grave if he could. They say she walks out there sometimes.'

'*Walks?* Why, Janet Bawtry, you great superstitious gowk, how can you believe such a thing?'

'Gowk's not ladylike,' she said automatically as she had when I was a child. She seemed to pull herself together. 'Happen you're reight. It could have been one of the girls off to meet a lad.'

When she had left the room I parted the curtain and peered out but could only see my own reflection against the yellow lamplight.

When I had calmed myself sufficiently to go down to the drawing-room again I found my aunt sitting there alone, looking distressed, for Courtney had gone out to see an old acquaintance in the district, or so he said.

I was relieved. I would have found it difficult to be

natural after what had been said between us, and wondered if he felt the same. I sat by her and began to thread her interminable embroidery needles, while, too upset to work, she first complained, then excused, then blamed Dyson, herself and me for not making him feel truly welcome, and then invented half a dozen excuses for his absence which neither of us quite believed. One thing was certain. In this respect he had not changed. He was as unpredictable and restless as ever.

CHAPTER FOUR

Courtney did not bring me a slave with a jewel in her nose or a white elephant as he had promised when I was thirteen, but he did produce a box of eastern fineries, saris, Kashmir shawls, trinkets and peacock feather fans.

I unpacked them one night after dinner and amused myself draping them around me. I could see he was watching me, and through the mirror I could see Dyson watching him with the old familiar wariness.

My ball would not be a very large affair, not more than a hundred people or so, but I was having my gown made by a Scarborough dressmaker and not by our local sewing woman.

I spread the violet and silver gauze over my white muslin dress, and said I thought I would have the sari made up into a ball dress.

'You will look magnificent,' said Courtney. 'An eastern princess.'

'I'm beginning to regret the white elephant. To make my entrance into the ballroom.'

'Ablaze with diamonds! Have you no jewels, Isabel?'

'There are plenty of jewels in the bank,' said my aunt, and at once looked reproachfully at Dyson. She had told me on many occasions that my father had spent a fortune on jewels for Maria-Amata.

'I will speak to Mr. Shawcross about getting a piece from the bank for you to wear for your ball,' said Dyson. 'I am sure he will allow.'

When he had gone she said angrily, 'Allow indeed! Who do they belong to, if not to you? Dyson takes too much upon himself.'

Actually he had been extremely good about my ball which was planned to celebrate my birthday in December and Courtney's return. I knew my aunt hoped to celebrate our engagement although she did not speak about it openly, and certainly never hinted it before Dyson. He regarded the ball as a public gesture which would recognise me as Sir Lockwood's daughter and silence forever the local gossip about my mother. Dyson watched my reputation as he had my education, with a dogged determination that the finished product should be the very best. I imagined this was from a mixture of family pride and his rigid sense of his duty towards me. I was not particularly grateful.

That summer I had dreamed of my ball, of waltzing in Courtney's arms to the envy of all my girl friends, and although the man who had returned was not the boy I had dreamed about, there was a touch of danger about him that I found very fascinating.

He was so handsome that he turned every woman's head. Sometimes he was my devoted beau, attentive and charming, sometimes he was abrupt and preoccupied, sometimes heavy-eyed and listless as though still suffering from the after effects of his fever. Often he was inexplicably absent.

I knew the light-hearted pursuits and innocuous gossip of my local friends bored him. He was worldly beyond our experience. The boys with whom we rode, danced and flirted seemed as callow as spring lambs beside his sophistication. He could be indifferent to the point of rudeness, yet he could charm when he wanted to. He charmed Mrs. Lister and May into ignoring the rumoured scandal they had heard and when I taxed him with it, he laughed at me. We were at Fieldhouse Grange, May's home, for one of Mrs. Lister's evening parties.

My aunt was playing bridge. Courtney had danced with me twice and spent the rest of the evening prowling round the card tables watching the play a little contemptuously, for the stakes were not high enough to tempt him. He told me he did not care 'to play cards' he liked to gamble. But in reality he was watching me.

He caught me after a set of lancers, took my arm and led me away to get an ice. He froze my poor partner, who had been intending to do the same thing, with an intimidating scowl. I was annoyed by his high-handedness and this started our argument. Courtney listened, his eyes glinting lazily, obviously amused at the rumours about his life in India.

'What frightful depravity am I accused of? Gambling?'

I nodded.

'And when have I not gambled? What else?'

I coloured. 'Other things.'

'Things too unmentionable for a well brought up young girl to mention?' He was goading me, in the old familiar way. He whispered theatrically in my ear, '*A woman?*'

'Yes.' I dug the spoon into my ice and put it down. He had always had a talent for provoking me. He said he liked to see my Spanish temper flare and my dark eyes flash.

'Well, well, *well*! So little Isabel expected me to live like a monk for six years.'

He got the explosion of temper that he had been trying for.

'Little Isabel expected you to live like a gentleman. The Listers' friend spoke of a native woman.'

His nonchalance cracked and he went white to the lips.

'If you tell me his name I'll thrash the lying young brute!'

I went on impetuously, telling him the thoughts I had kept to myself since his return.

'I don't believe it and if I did I would not care. I am not concerned with what you've done, but only what you are now and what you intend to do.' I stopped abruptly, realising how blatantly I was exposing myself. I was no longer thirteen to blurt out my heart's desires. His voice was unsteady when he spoke to me.

'I do believe you really mean it. What a strange creature you are, Isabel.'

'Strange?' I repeated. 'I am only an ordinary girl.'

'How old are you? Nearly nineteen?' He made a gesture towards the ballroom. 'One moment you are playing the fool with these children, and the next you are a woman, magnificent, burning me with those great eyes until you drive me mad. I think your mother was a witch and not a dancer, and you've learned her spells!' My amazed face made him realise what he was saying. He turned away, saying roughly. 'Make my apologies to Mama and Mrs. Lister. I cannot stand this sort of entertainment.'

He called for his hat and coat and left me standing there uncertain whether to be furious or triumphant. He would be away for a whole day, a whole evening — sometimes days together. I did not know if his mother or Dyson questioned him as to where he went, but I could not bring myself to do so.

I was vividly conscious of him all the time. I felt my mother's blood within me. She filled my imagination these days and sometimes it seemed she was teaching me to exploit my beauty from her grave.

There was a story of her dancing in the great hall after dinner, lifted on to the long oak refectory table which stood there, her eyes flashing, her long black hair shaking down over her white shoulders, castanets and heels beating out the cross rhythm of the flamenco. 'Like to drive a man mad,' Oldroyd had said. 'Sometimes she would flick a man's glass out of his hand with the tip of her red shoes. You should have heard them shouting for her . . . but no man dared touch her, or Sir Lockwood would have killed him, I do believe.' So I began to wonder if I were too like her, a woman a man might desire but not want to marry, and having married, not want to acknowledge. So whenever I was with Courtney I glinted and gleamed, and watched him kindle, using every ruse in my limited experience to make him declare himself, every evasion and rejection increasing my will that he should love me and tell me so.

The tension between Courtney and me was such that I felt sure that everyone must see.

One day in November I went to the meet over at Norland with Oldroyd in attendance. My care of Bantry had miscarried — Courtney did not care to ride or hunt with me as he had when we were younger, and this particular week he had been avoiding me.

The fox went a long way inland, and it was mid-afternoon and cold, with the sun westering as Oldroyd and I hacked back across the fields to Sutherdyke. On the main Filey Road some miles from Sutherdyke, The Crown Inn stands at a crossroad overlooking a triangular piece of greensward called Norhead Green — The Crown where Courtney used to go as a boy to escape Dyson's discipline or his mother's reproaches. The place had a bad name locally, the country folk made lewd jokes about it. It was said to be the centre of the illegal cock-fighting fraternity and a meeting place for gypsies, horse copers and thieves. Its landlord, a man called Swathe, had once been a seaman, and many foreign sailors from Hull found their way there, believed to be engaged in the smuggling trade. I pulled up my mount as Oldroyd bent to unlatch the gate leading to the road, and I saw one of the Sutherdyke traps outside the inn. There was no mistaking it. All our vehicles were of a distinctive dark green, with a small crest on the door panels. Oldroyd followed my glance, and looked uncomfortable.

'Did Mr. Courtney ask for that trap to be harnessed for him before we left?'

'Well, Miss Isabel, I can't say. Young gentlemen have their own amusement . . . it's no real harm. A place for coursing, cock-fighting and betting, is t'Crown . . .'

I thought of the whispered rumours I had heard from May Lister and Janet had told me of the sort of women that frequented The Crown. I put my heel to Ladybird, and was off across the field, over a fence and into the open country towards Sutherdyke, leaving Oldroyd calling after me. I got back on the road by a lane just before the level crossing at Norland Halt. The gates were closed, and the crossing keeper's wife was standing at her cottage door holding a little boy in her arms. He was crying loudly. He was an unusual little boy. He had an olive-skinned, heart-shaped face with big hazel eyes — I could not remember ever seeing such eyelashes on a child. He stopped crying and stared at my horse. He was dressed in a white serge sailor suit and thin patent shoes in spite of the bitter day, and he was certainly no cottage-child.

I reined in and spoke to the woman, whom I knew.

'What's the matter? Is he lost?'

'Aye,' she answered. 'It's t'little lad from Ivy Lodge. The new folk. He wandered down on t'line. Gave me a reight turn. Will you tek him back, Miss Broadbent? I must stay with the gates.'

'Of course I will. Have you got something to put round him?' He was shivering with the cold.

The woman handed him up to me on the front of the saddle, and fetched a shawl. He was so light and slight it was like handling a bird. He gazed up at me with his huge eyes.

'What's your name?' I asked.

'Andrew,' he said. 'Will you, lady, please take me to my home?'

His accent was strange. Something in the way he formed the sentence, rather than the actual sound that was so foreign. I held Ladybird in while the train clattered past and the woman turned the wheel to open the gates .

'It is a big horse,' he said. 'I have never been on a big horse before. It is bigger than a hathi.'

'What is a hathi?'

'An elephant,' he translated.

'What language is that — hathi?'

'It is what the people speak,' he said.

'And you speak it too?'

'I speak it with my ayah, but with my mama I speak English, because she is a *mem-sahib* and they all speak English.'

'What is your second name?'

'McAllister. I am Andrew McAllister.'

'But that sounds Scottish.'

'What is Scottish?' he asked solemnly. He was warmer now, wrapped in the thick shawl, and he smiled at me with beautiful white teeth like split almonds. I touched up Ladybird, and I felt his small heart quicken as the horse broke into a trot. He had wandered quite a long way for such a small boy and it took me quite ten minutes to get to Ivy Lodge.

As I drew rein a young woman came running down the drive calling the child's name. She was very slender and pale, and her eyes two pools of blackness fringed with enormous silky lashes. Apart from her eyes she was not good-looking. She was painfully thin and worn-looking, her lower face rather weak, her teeth prominent. The blue and yellow checked afternoon dress she wore was too thin for such a cold day and hung about her as though she had lost weight since it was made. Her hair blew about her face in the wind and she tried to control it with delicate, ineffectual hands. I noticed the curious colour of the half-moons of her finger-nails — a dark hue, almost like a bruise.

On seeing us she opened the gate and ran out into the road stretching up her arms for the boy. I gave him to her, and she hugged him against her breast half-crying with relief.

'Oh, Andrew, you are so naughty. I could not find you. Janhoo and I have been searching the whole house and the gardens for you. Where have you been?'

He grinned up at me mischievously, safe in his mother's arms.

'He *is* naughty!' I tried to sound stern. 'The crossing keeper's wife found him on the lines. Big trains can run over little boys, Andrew.'

'Oh heavens,' she cried. 'He might have been killed.'

A thin elderly Indian woman dressed in her native clothes, with a grey West Riding woollen shawl wrapped incongruously over her head and shoulders came slip-slopping down the drive. She was very dark-skinned, with dull glazed eyes and the cold made her look like a sad, wizened old monkey.

The young woman must be Mrs. McAllister, the new tenant of Ivy Lodge. With the child clasped in her arms she turned and in a language I could not understand spoke angrily to her servant, who wailed, covered her face, bending nearly double in her distress.

Mrs. McAllister glanced at my startled face, and then said in English with the same lilting accent as the small boy, 'She is such a fool. She gets worse. She would die for

86

him but she has not the sense to keep him off the road. All right, Janhoo — *jao*!'

The Indian woman straightened up and drew the shawl closer round her, looking at me with such an expression of hatred and fury that I was startled. There was something personal about it, although I had never set eyes on her before. It was as though in some way she held me and not her own carelessness as responsible for Andrew's escapade. She turned back to the house, her heelless shoes flapping and her feet, clad in a pair of grey men's socks, ridiculous below her bunched muslin skirts.

'Janhoo looks like an old grey hen!' said Andrew and roared with laughter. 'She was bad to permit me to run away.'

'You were bad to do so,' said his mother. 'Now thank this lady for finding you and bringing you home to Mama.'

'Thank you, lady,' he said, with his delightful, impertinent smile.

'I thank you myself, from my heart,' said his mother.

'You must be Mrs. McAllister,' I said. 'Are you from India? My cousin Courtney has not long come back from India.'

'Your cousin?'

'I'm Isabel Broadbent.'

She stared up at me, and said '*So!* But I was told that you were . . .' She stopped, and said confusedly, 'I was not told that you were so beautiful.'

I laughed. 'It sounds as though someone has told you I was rather ugly. How horrid of them. I must go. Perhaps I may call to see you some time in the future to enquire after Andrew?'

She cried out, 'No!' and set the boy down in a panic, her dark face clouded with distress. 'Andrew. Go into the house.'

He looked rebellious but this was a tone he knew he had to obey. He too looked an odd little figure pattering down the curved, tree-shadowed drive to the house, the shawl trailing on the ground. Mrs. McAllister came up to me, her hand on the pommel of my saddle, her face upturned to mine in desperation. 'Miss Broadbent,' she said, 'I must ask you please not to visit me here.'

'As you like,' I replied, chagrined. I had made the offer in goodwill, thinking she might be lonely, a newcomer to the district, and I was not used to having a social approach refused point blank.

She was aware of my feelings — the plain, sallow face was acutely sensitive. 'It sounds discourteous, I know. It is a matter I cannot explain. My advisers have asked me particularly not to have any callers while I am here. It will only be a short while. It is a matter of — of legal settlement that I am here for. To put it briefly, the opposing party does not know I am in England. I thank you for what you did today, but I pray that you will not visit me.'

'As you like,' I said again, slightly mollified. 'I do not wish to intrude. Will you send the shawl back to the gate-keeper's wife — and thank her, for it was she who really rescued the little boy?'

I touched up Ladybird and jogged off down the road on the four-mile ride back to Sutherdyke. The strangeness and mystery of this encounter occupied my mind, so that I temporarily forgot my angry suspicions about Courtney. The sky had cleared as it so often did with the evening tide, and I loved this East Riding country. Mounted on Ladybird I could see far across the land. The sea on the left, and on the right the wolds rolling gently away, with the windmills and the church spires standing up over the cornfields, bare at this time of the year with the crows tumbling homeward in the wind. The little villages seemed to nestle in hollows as though sheltering from the great north-easterly gales that so often blew from the North Sea. I loved the harshness and simplicity — and one day, as far as I could see, it would be mine.

I went up to my room and rang for Janet who soon had a bathful of hot water before the bedroom fire.

As she helped me off with my boots, and laid out an afternoon dress, she told me that Dyson would not be home until the evening, and that my aunt was in 'a fair tizzy' about Courtney, who had left the house in the morning and not returned to lunch with her as she had expected.

'Happen he'll turn up like a bad penny,' she said laconically, pouring the warm water over my back. 'And what's this about you galloping off and leaving Oldroyd? He's in a high old state — I reckon Mr. Dyson will have something to say to that.'

'Oldroyd won't tell him,' I said confidently. I thought of the green trap outside The Crown but said nothing to Janet. If Courtney preferred to spend the day in low company rather than riding with me, I did not want her to know.

My aunt was waiting for me in the drawing-room, the tea tray on a small table beside her. She poured me a cup, and waited until Hawkins had left the room before asking if I had seen Courtney. I said I had not seen him, but I knew where he was and I told her. She did not appear in the least shocked or surprised.

'Poor boy. He is not well enough to ride with you yet. The fever is very enervating. Cannot you see how languid he is sometimes?'

'If he is not well, why does he not say so? He finds my company so boring that he has to go to a place like The Crown for diversion.'

'Have you ever thought that you might be driving him beyond endurance?'

She rose. At that hour she always went to her room to rest. 'He seems to be deeply in love with you — indeed sometimes when he speaks to me about you he sounds like my unfortunate brother raving over your mother.'

She automatically collected the bits and pieces that she inevitably carried, and I, just as automatically, helped her. Lace handkerchief, lorgnettes, reticule and her small glass phial of perfumed smelling salts.

'If that is true — why doesn't he speak to me?' I said.

'Because Dyson has forbidden it.'

I was outraged.

'But Dyson has no right to do so.'

'Nevertheless,' said my aunt, 'he has forbidden Courtney to speak to you of marriage until you are of age.'

I opened the door for her and she went up to her room. I stood there alone. The great house seemed to close down on me. Often, in this mood, I would walk over to Monkstonby to the Bawtrys' cottage and sit with Bessy for an hour or so. I still called her Aunt Bessy. Her flat common sense and dry Yorkshire simplicity were like a tonic to me. 'It's thy road, and tha've got to find t'best way of treading it,' she would say. 'You didn't like being a common lass — it's no manner of use wailing now because you've been turned into a lady.'

But it was too late to go to Monkstonby now — the low November sun was already touching the smoky roofs of the town. I took my thick plaid cloak from the hall cupboard, pulled the hood up about my head and went out into the garden.

It was very still now, the frost beginning to whiten the ground again and the winter light just failing. I went along one of the grass alleys between the yew hedges, flanked by the beds of spindly, frost-browned roses. I walked quickly, out beyond the garden, through the paddock to the low cliff above the beach, watched the winter sea, grey and forbidding, saw the lighthouse on Norhead begin to flash its nightly warning. I felt lonely and bewildered; I needed affection and advice and had no one to whom I could turn.

A sea mist was rolling in as I went back towards the house. As I re-entered the rose-alley it was nearly dark. I thought I heard a faint metallic clickety sound and stopped to listen, but could hear nothing. It could be the distant sound of harness from the stables, but I did not think so. As I began to walk I was certain I heard it again, and a faint rustle of leaves, as though someone was walking level with me on the other side of the thick yew hedge, stopping when I stopped, starting when I started, and occasionally something, I knew not what, making this nearly inaudible sound. I remembered the tales of my mother, dragging out the last days of her frustrated young life there in the rose-garden. Telling her rosary beads, playing with her castanets, faintly rattling and clicking in her exhausted hands. I had been high-handed with Janet about her superstitious fears, but now I panicked, turned down a side alley and fled headlong, out of the garden, through a plantation of larches and firs, over a stile, bursting out on to the main road almost under the hooves of a trap that came bowling along from the direction of Monkstonby, lights bobbing through the mist.

The horse was jerked to a clattering halt, and above my head in the mist I heard Dyson bark, '*Isabel!* What the devil are you doing out here alone on a night like this?'

His voice and manner held suspicion.

'Were you going to meet someone?'

'No!' I flared. 'I thought I heard someone in the rose-garden and was afraid.'

'And was there someone?'

'I don't know.'

'Did you see anyone?'

'No,' I said, my fear disappearing in my resentment, remembering what had sent me rushing out into the dusk.

'Get in at once,' he said. 'You have no business to be wandering out at night alone.'

He put out a hand and hauled me up beside him, flicking the pony into a trot. If I had had any idea of telling him any more about my eerie experience in the rose-garden it went right out of my head. I remembered what my aunt had told me and sat simmering with anger. He turned the trap into the drive, and said more kindly, 'Don't glower, Isabel. You know it's a foolhardy thing to go out alone after sundown. You get trampers and mumping fellows along this road at night.'

'It was not sundown when I left the house and I can go out by myself if I want to. But I am glad to have this chance of speaking to you. By what right have you forbidden Courtney to speak to me?'

'Of marriage?'

'Yes.'

'Who said this?'

'Your mother. Is it true?'

'Yes, it's true. You were bought to Sutherdyke on my responsibility. I am your guardian and I have a duty to you, as you have to yourself.'

'I have a right to happiness.'

'It is not a thing to be secured by rights as your father discovered.'

I said illogically, 'You are not my father and Aunt Rose says you are interested in me yourself.'

Immediately I had said it I knew it was an awful thing to say, but it was said, and I could not withdraw. I have a vivid memory of his face beneath the high hat against the scurrying background of leafless trees.

'My mother seems to know more about the state of my affections than I do myself.'

92

'I understand it is not a question of affection,' I went on recklessly, throwing the unforgivable words at him. 'It is a question of my money.'

The horse trotted to a standstill in the stable-yard, steaming under the lights. Dyson got wearily down — he did not turn to help me as Courtney would have, but stood there in the flickering lantern lights, a huge menacing figure in his caped coat. I scrambled out of the trap, and the groom led the horse away. I was very afraid.

'And you believe all this romantic rubbish?' he said.

'I cannot understand why else you should forbid Courtney to speak. As your mother says, you have always disliked and been jealous of him. You cannot bear him to have something you cannot.'

Dyson gave a short bark of laughter.

'You can believe what you damned well like,' he said. 'You are a child and a fool. When you are of age you can go to the devil with any man you choose, but while you are my responsibility you will do as I say if I have to shut you up in your room to make you obedient.'

He turned and without another word strode off into the house.

I flew up into my room and burst into tears of fury. A hundred wild plans to defeat and humiliate Dyson went through my head. When Janet came in to draw the curtains and light the lamps she brought a note from Courtney asking me to come down early and meet him in the winter-garden before dinner. At first, I thought I would not go, and then, remembering my aunt's words, 'Have you ever thought you might be driving him beyond endurance?' a sudden wild resolve came into my mind.

When I slipped quietly into the winter-garden he was waiting for me in the warm darkness. The caged birds chirruped sleepily among the plants and outside the winter darkness pressed against the steamy glass. I went straight to him and we stood for a moment, looking at each other in the half light. There was a persistent scent, sweet and heavy although very faint, which seemed to come from the pale orchids blooming in the dusk.

He put his arms about me with a sound like a groan, and drew me against him and our mouths touched and then clung, and any lingering scrap of caution burned away like paper in a flame.

'Isabel,' he said. 'Isabel. I have been longing to do this.'

'And why didn't you?' I said against his searching lips. 'Because of Dyson?'

I felt him hesitate, and then he spoke in a tone I had never heard before. 'No — because of myself.'

I drew back and he caught me against him. 'Don't look like that. I love you. I am no good to you. Dyson is a bully and a boor and I lothe him, but in a way he is right. It would be better if I went away and never saw you again.'

He stroked the hair back from my forehead.

'It isn't just the memory of a childish infatuation, is it, Isabel? I must know what you really feel.'

It was what I had wanted to hear above all things. His arrogance was broken and he was pleading with me. I knew what it was to desire and be desired. But hard within me was that core of Broadbent stubbornness and reckless pride. Now I knew that Courtney loved me Dyson would learn that he was not my master.

'I will tell you what I feel, Courtney, and what you mean to me.' I drew in my breath and told him of my wonderful, daring, mad idea. 'If you will take me away from here, I will come with you. If you want me to be your wife, why should we wait for two years? If I was your wife no one could separate us.'

He said, almost inaudibly, 'God help me,' and I flashed at him, touchy and proud as ever, 'You said you loved me.

94

Do you not want me to be your wife? Are you ashamed of me?'

'No, Isabel, no . . .'

'Are you afraid? Are you afraid of Dyson, like everyone in this house?'

He held my hands behind me and kissed my angry face until my suspicions and defiance melted into joy.

'Just now I am afraid of you,' he said. 'You drive me insane. What are you asking? You are only nineteen. Dyson and Mr. Shawcross are your legal guardians. You cannot marry without their consent.'

'In Scotland I can,' I said triumphantly. 'When I was at school one of the girls was going to run off, but her parents found out and stopped it. But she told us her plans. In Scotland if one can stay for fourteen days one can get married at my age . . .' I faltered, because his face seemed terrible to me, as though he was suffering some tangible pain. 'We are near Hull. Steamers go from Hull to Aberdeen. It would be quite easy.' I touched his cheeks with my lips tentatively, pleadingly and he held me very close.

'Yes,' he said, 'yes'. You are wonderful and strange. I have wasted my life dreaming but you would make your dreams reality.'

'Dyson is going to send me away to London after Christmas. I am to have six months there with May Lister and her family. He tells me I should meet a lot of people, but what he means is that I should find a suitable husband. I will never marry anyone but you. He would send me away at once if he saw us together like this. If you will take me away, Courtney, it must be just after my ball. London is a long way from Scotland.'

'Isabel — you are quite, quite sure? You know little about me. I have been a thoughtless fool. A criminal fool.'

'With money?'

'With money — and other things. You have heard stories about me which are not true, but there are many things I have done which I would not want you to know.'

'I told you I did not care what you have been, so long as you love me now. And when I am twenty-one we shall have no money worries. We shall only have to love each other and do as we like.'

'You child,' he said. 'You wild thing. But you are right. It's too easy to be hopeless and give up. We will do this, and I will plan everything. I promise you. We will be married.'

'We are to be married,' I cried like a child. 'We are engaged.'

'Look.' He took a twisted tendril from one of the vines, and very delicately wound it round my finger. 'Look at my hands. I am trembling — there — a ring until I can give you a real jewel.'

I kissed it, slipped it off, opened the locket that I wore and put it inside.

'We must tell no one, Isabel. Not my mother or Janet — or your friend May Lister. When I have completed our plans I will tell you. I may have to go away, because I must raise some money, and book our passages to Scotland, and find somewhere there where we can stay in secret until we are married.'

'You think Dyson will follow us?'

'I think he might.'

I wish we were going tonight.'

He kissed me again, and as my head fell back against his shoulder I saw something move and vanish in the dark night outside, and cried out.

'Courtney, there is someone there! There is someone outside watching us ... there again, towards the rose-garden ...'

Courtney let me go so quickly that I nearly stumbled,

opened the door and plunged out into the damp November mist. I peered fearfully out into the garden, remembering the unseen presence which had sent me flying out into the main road nearly under the horse's hooves earlier that night. I was certain this time that there had been a presence out there in the garden sliding away, like a fish into the weeds, at my cry. The sea mist was milky now in the light of a newly risen moon, but I could see no one, hear no sound but Courtney's returning footsteps on the gravel and the distant hoot of an owl.

He came in, closed and locked the door.

'There is no one there.'

'It must be the ghost,' I said, and tried to laugh, and when he questioned me sharply told him of the white figure Janet had seen in the rose-garden on the night of his return. 'They say it is my mother's ghost ... maybe she materialised to warn me against you.'

He put his arm round my shoulder, glancing round the glass walls that gleamed between the plants and creepers.

'Come inside. This place seems to be ringed with eyes.' He took me through into the white-panelled morning-room. The lamps were lit in there making a cheerful glow. He drew the curtains across the french windows, and the sound of the dinner gong boomed from the hall.

'Promise me, Isabel, that you will not go outside alone at night.'

'That is what Dyson said to me this evening.' I told him of my experience in the rose-garden, the suspicion that I was being followed, the evasive little sound beyond the hedge, and faltered because his face was so strained and strange. Under the lamps his pupils were like pin-points in the pure transparent blue of his eyes.

'Don't look like that,' I cried. 'It could have been some animal — a cat or rat, a fox or squirrel. I could have imagined the whole thing.'

'Dyson was quite right. You must not go out at night alone. Not even in the grounds.'

'But what danger could there be?'

'The expectation of a great fortune is a danger in itself. You will promise me?'

'Courtney,' I asked suddenly, 'why do you go to The Crown at Norhead Green?'

He looked at me, and with a savage shift of mood, 'Have you been spying on me?'

'No. I was riding. I saw a Sutherdyke trap outside The Crown. I guessed you were there.'

'And why do you imagine I go there?'

'I — I don't know,' I faltered, then burst out, 'I thought perhaps there was some girl there . . .'

His fierce suspicion vanished. He threw back his head, laughed and drew me against him.

'There is no other girl for me but you. Since I have been home I do not see other women. Do you think it has been easy for me to be here, so near you, living in the same house and not daring to touch you or tell you what I feel? I go there because there is nowhere else. Swathe, the landlord, is an amusing ruffian and I get sick of your milk-and-water local society. These Yorkshire squires bore me to extinction. The prices of grain, wool, and mutton and coal — and the eternal talk of the weather. God, what conversation. I have to get away from it.'

'But now it will be different,' I said, and twined my hand in his and he kissed me again. 'Now we know and are together. Now I know you love me. We shall have plans to make.' Outside in the hall the gong sounded a second impatient summons. 'We must go in to dinner.'

'My darling,' he said, and let me go. 'Go ahead of me, as though you have come from your room. We have a secret to keep. It would be better if we did not go in together.'

I went alone into the empty hall, ran silently up to the first landing, then turned and descended as though I was just coming from my room. I became aware that Dyson was standing in the library doorway watching the manoeuvre, rubbing his upper lip with unsmiling gravity. I felt the blood fly to my cheeks. I stooped, pretended to retrieve my handkerchief from one of the steps, straightened up.

'I dropped my handkerchief.'

'I thought,' he said, 'there must be some explanation.'

I went down quickly and he followed me into the dining-room. My aunt was already there, and almost at once Courtney came in, and took the place opposite me. He looked changed, young again, gay and smiling, and the transparent blue eyes teased and challenged me across the table as they had six years ago.

I was very young and wildly in love, and now there was this great secret between us. It was exciting and amusing to play our game beneath their noses without giving ourselves away. It was like the old days, when we used to plot and scheme together to get away on our own.

That evening Dyson stayed in the drawing-room for over an hour. He did not talk very much but his large, silent presence was irksome to us — we were willing that he should leave the room and go back to the library and his dull account books. I dare not look at Courtney for fear of betraying myself, and it was nearly ten when Dyson finally rose.

I always had the feeling that he could see beneath the surface of everything. I knew he had a way of waiting until his opponent grew careless and gave him the advantage — I had seen him do this often in the days when he used to take me with him to Leeds on business. I forced myself to be calm and circumspect while he was there.

As he rose, my aunt said, 'They tell me that the new

tenant at Ivy Lodge comes from India, Courtney.'

'Why should you imagine I should be interested? You know I hate the country.'

'I know, but it is unusual. Local people seem to think the lady has Indian blood.'

Reminded, I burst in with my small adventure.

'I met Mrs. McAllister this afternoon,' I said. 'She is no darker skinned than I am — only, perhaps, her hands. Now I remember her finger-nails were dark — sort of bluish.'

'The certain mark of the Eurasian,' Courtney said. 'One can believe them to be Europeans — until one sees their hands. You must not know this woman, Isabel.'

He was deadly serious. I was astounded.

'If you have lived in the East as I have you will know that the half-caste is the lowest form of life. Lying, cheating, crawling people, insinuating their way in where they are not wanted, and contaminating everything they touch.'

'Well, this lady made it pretty obvious that she did not wish to know me,' I said. 'Indeed although she was glad to have her little boy back, she seemed to be quite dismayed at my presence. I don't particularly want to know her and certainly had no encouragement to do so.'

'You think I'm unreasonable. I assure you I am not. In India the two races do not mix. I have been robbed by such people. Money-lenders and thieves. I have known our fellows out there be ruined by making marriages with the women. We do not want to receive such people at Sutherdyke.'

'Indeed not!' said my aunt, ranging herself at once on his side, and looking reproachfully at Dyson. 'It is bad enough that they should be allowed to settle in the district — and on our property.'

'On Isabel's property,' he corrected her gently. She

looked ruffled, hating to be reminded of it. 'And the lady is not our tenant. I could not prevent the lease-owners sub-letting and I would not have done so had I been able. For all Courtney's racial prejudices she seems a harmless, nervous creature by all accounts and is doing no one any harm.'

'If what Isabel says is true, the lady is probably the usual bazaar scum,' said Courtney. 'They harm like snakes — striking in the dark.'

I thought he was unreasonable and could see no harm in the mild untidy-looking Mrs. McAllister. I thought he must have some personal reason for his feeling that he had not spoken of. But if this was so he made no attempt to explain.

Dyson went to the library to work and after he had gone we had a pleasant evening. We played the piano and sang, and played backgammon — Courtney was in his most charming mood and put himself out to please his mother and myself, and free from Dyson's cool and observant eyes, our hands and glances could meet and our lips too, briefly, behind my aunt's back. It was a happy evening — innocent, as though we were young lovers who had just met, just declared their love. He was so different, and sounded so happy. My aunt glowed in his presence, pretended not to see our affection and forget her complaints and resentments. I could see she thought our future was settled, and that brief, happy evening, I thought so too.

It was nearly midnight when I went upstairs. Courtney opened the drawing-room door and followed me out into the hall. We dare not embrace — we stood there close, our hands touching, the silence pregnant with desire.

'Good night,' he whispered, 'good night my darling . . .'

'Good night, Courtney . . . my love . . .'

I went upstairs to my room and as I reached the upper

gallery I heard the library door open and Dyson's voice asking Courtney to come to him.

I was too excited to go to bed. I never kept Janet up late to help me as my aunt kept her maid, but she had laid out my night things, so I undressed, put on a wrap and slippers, and sat before the fire. If I had kept a diary like my friend May Lister I would have written my heart into it that night. I wandered about the room, brushed and plaited my long black hair, tried to read a novel, peered fearfully between the curtains at the rose-garden, grey and black in the misty moonlight. I thought of Courtney's words 'A great fortune is a danger in itself,' and wondered what he had meant. But nothing stirred outside now.

I became aware of the murmuring of men's voices in the library below my room and now they rose to the vicious crescendo of a quarrel and then I heard the heavy sound of furniture falling and the hysterical barking of Dyson's spaniel bitch.

I ran down into the hall and found my aunt standing outside the library door, white and trembling, listening to the noise inside.

'They are fighting,' she whispered. 'Isabel — they are fighting.'

Hawkins came from the kitchen quarters, his Cockney face sharp with curiosity and other servants, apprehensive but inquisitive, began to creep into the hall.

Behind the heavy door Courtney's voice could be heard shouting, 'I'll kill you — I'll kill you one day. What I do is my own business and you have no right to question me.'

There was the sound of a struggle, and then a cry, and the door flew open and Courtney, panting, tie loose, a bruise across his bleeding lips, stood staring at us as though he had never seen us before. His mother ran to him, but he thrust her aside and went across the hall to the main door, plunging out into the night like a drunken man.

CHAPTER FIVE

Dyson came to the door of the library.

'Get off back to your quarters. Tell your people to go about their business and stop gauping,' he said to Hawkins, and the little crowd of curious servants fled like scurrying mice.

He looked at my aunt and said, 'Mother — go upstairs. Isabel, I wish to speak with you.'

'Have you tried to murder him?' my aunt cried. 'Was it about money again? You are jealous of him, you always have been because of my preference . . .'

'Mother, don't let's have that old song again,' he said wearily. 'Go to bed. Isabel, come here.'

I followed him into the library, and he sat down at his desk. He had been holding a handkerchief round his wrist, and now he took it away and I could see a jagged cut on the back of his hand. He kept bandages and medical supplies in a drawer for any minor accident in the house. I stood on the other side of his desk and watched him methodically binding his wrist. On the desk before us lay a turquoise-handled Indian dagger not much bigger than a penknife, which I knew belonged to Courtney.

When he had finished Dyson held out his wrist, and asked me to tie the ends of the bandage, which I did with trembling fingers, knowing he was watching me, not daring to look up and meet his eyes.

When the ends of the bandage were tied, he dropped it

into the drawer in front of his desk with an expression of distaste.

'He didn't try to kill you?' I said.

'Let us say, he threatened to. I do not kill so easily.'

'But why?'

'Because I would not let him have something he wants very much.'

'He must have been terribly provoked.'

'Yes — maybe,' he said, and the dreadful waiting silence closed down again.

'Can I go?' I said pleadingly. I was frightened and bewildered and I did not want him to question me.

'No!' He waited again, and then said, 'Well, let's hear what you have to say, Isabel.'

'About what?'

'About Courtney.'

If his tone had been different I might have talked to him and he might have helped me, but his voice and manner were an insult so, instead of answering, I flashed an accusation.

'I think my aunt is right. You do want him out of the way. You pretend to be upright and honest but you really want my fortune for yourself.'

He stood up and came round the desk and picked me up in his great arms, and kissed me. I was too astounded to struggle or scream. The hard mouth came down on mine and my senses reeled beneath the probing lips. When he put me down I nearly fell.

'You great brute,' I shouted. 'You great big lubberly brute.'

'That sounds more like Monkstonby Quay,' he said. 'That's to teach you that one kiss is like another at your age. I could have played Courtney's sly game these past years, if I had wanted to, and then, likely, you'd have been hanging round my neck.'

I was beside myself. 'How dare you! How dare you!'

'How dare you behave like a slut? I told you to watch your ways and keep away from Courtney until you were of age. Do you think I haven't seen your ways — glancing at him, flirting, tempting, leading him on. And don't you suppose if Courtney were not there it would be another man, even me? Why don't you get up on the table and dance like your mother, if that's the sort of admiration you want?'

I was crying with speechless rage.

'You're going to London with the Listers the minute this ball of yours is over. I agreed to it to introduce you to the county as the future owner of Sutherdyke — so don't behave like a gypsy dancing for pennies outside the inns, or a fisher lass brawling on the quays!' He went back behind his desk. 'After this ball the farther you are away from my mother's persuasions the better. You think of her as your ally. I tell you she thinks of nothing but your fortune for her lovely boy.' He picked up a pen and threw it down violently, it stuck quivering in the polished oak. 'Faugh!' he said. 'They make me sick with their avarice.'

'Courtney is not like that. You only say it because you hate him.'

'You know no more of Courtney than you do of me. You are a child and know nothing of life or men. In London you will meet a hundred pretty fellows who will be after your money and your beauty, and then you will see how you will fare. If you know the true from the counterfeit — prefer one kiss to another.'

He looked up and I was frightened by the blaze of his eyes. I had seen him angry, but never like this. He seemed filled with disgust of Courtney, me, his mother, and perhaps himself. 'Do you think I would not throw you and the whole estate into the hands of the first worthy man who asked for you if I could? Do you think I like playing factor and wet-nurse to you?'

'Oh, I hate you, Dyson Somerby. I wish I'd never seen you or Sutherdyke. I wish you'd left me at the cottage with Bessy Bawtry.'

'Aye,' his face changed sombrely. 'Aye — it might have been better for us all if we had never set eyes on you.'

He rose and walked to the door as though the springy strength of his big body was weighed down by a heavy burden and went out and left me alone, shaken, bewildered by emotions I did not understand. The big house was very silent now. The spaniel Sally lay shivering on the hearth, whining anxiously. I stroked her with a fellow feeling for her uncomprehending anxiety, and presently crept upstairs to my room.

I did not sleep well, dozing in a restless half sleep filled with threatening dreams, and as soon as the winter sky greyed with dawn, I lit a candle, and drew the curtains. At once I heard a step outside and gravel thrown against the window. Courtney stood below. He was wearing a heavy travelling coat and a tweed shooting hat, gloved and booted as though for a journey. He beckoned to me to come down.

I put on shoes and my thick, plaid, hooded cloak and went down the great staircase. Far away in the kitchens was a faint clatter and hiss of pipes, the early maids laying the trays, drawing the water to heat for the bedrooms. The light filtering through the great oriel touched the gilded picture frames and the cold polish of armour with shafts of amber, purple and crimson. The fires were not yet lit and it was cold. I went through the breakfast-room into the winter-garden and drew the bolts, and the bitter air caught my breath as I went out. He was waiting under the yew arch that led to the rose-garden and I ran across and was in his arms, and the nightmare faded and I was safe again, until I saw the bruise, livid on his pale face.

'Oldroyd has the trap ready,' he said. 'He is driving me to the station to catch the early train. I cannot live under the same roof as Dyson. It is impossible.'

'But you will come back?'

He put his arms closely round me and I brushed my lips gently against his, not wishing to hurt him.

'I am going to make you my wife, Isabel. Dyson can do nothing when you are my wife.' He glanced about him, as though he was afraid we were being watched or overheard. 'Don't fight him, Isabel. Pretend to be obedient. Don't defy him — agree to anything while I make my plans. I will come for you, I promise, and when I come I will have everything planned and ready. We will show him that he is not master of Sutherdyke or of you.'

It was these words as much as his kiss that moved me. If there was one thing I wanted to do it was this.

'Where are you going?'

'I must go to London, and then to Hull. We shall need money, for our journey, and to live — we shall have to live very simply for the next two years. I must raise some money.'

'But my ball — ' I said childishly, 'you will return for my ball? I am going to be sent to London with the Listers as soon as it is over.'

'That is when I shall return.'

He lifted one of my long black plaits of hair.

'This morning you look like the little girl who promised to wait until I returned from India. I wish to God I had never gone.'

'I wish so too.'

'You are sure about this, Isabel? You are sure you love me and this is what you want?'

'Quite sure.'

There was something so desperately sad about his voice

and eyes that I was full of tenderness towards him.

'Nothing is changed,' I said.

'Everything is changed, you and I most of all. Now, I must go. I will return for your birthday, and when I return you must be ready to go with me. I will not write to you. It would rouse suspicion. But I promise I will come.'

He kissed me once again and then he went. I heard his footsteps on the gravel, and presently the sound of wheels and hooves going down the drive to the main road.

The sun tipped the horizon turning the rimed, frosty world to a glitter of silver. It was still, cold and very beautiful. I went into the rose-garden. The fountain basin was coated with ice and the grey stone cupid clothed in frozen spears. The roses, almost leafless, carried scarlet seed vessels and brown buds that would never flower. I heard a sound, and turned sharply, but it was immediately stilled. A small, clicking metallic sound. A horse in its stall? A cat with a bell? A stableboy with a pail? The ghost? A dawn ghost? Rosary beads? Castanets? Ghosts were supposed to have clanking chains. This must be a very small ghost. I smiled to myself. In the daylight I was not afraid.

I went to the entrance of one of the rose-alleys that radiated from the fountain and looked along it, but nothing stirred save foraging birds and a dead leaf or so falling slowly through the still air. But then I remembered the movement in the darkness outside the winter-garden last night when I had been in Courtney's arms. Had someone watched our loving again this morning as we said good-bye?

I drew my hood closely about me and hurried back to the house.

The time before my ball in December went by with outward normality, although our inner tension showed in many ways. My aunt's impatience over any small upset, her bitter resentment towards Dyson because Courtney had gone away, and Dyson's manner, avoiding our company as much as possible, terse and preoccupied when he could not avoid it. Occasionally I would know he was watching me, rubbing that long, stubborn upper lip with his thumbnail. Although I planned secretly against him, I could not meet his eyes.

I knew his words had been wiser than I would admit, though his way of making me understand them had been coarse and brutal. He thought I was in love with love, and that my impetuosity was reckless and dangerous. But I would prove him wrong. Courtney and I were young, we loved each other passionately, we would force him to give us our freedom and happiness. I waited with a single-minded longing for the day when Courtney would take me away, and in that time of waiting often tried to create an image of my handsome young love in my mind — but somehow all I could remember of him were those transparent blue eyes in the bruised face, pin-pointed with hatred for Dyson.

Courtney had said, 'We will show him he is not our master,' and it was what I had wanted him to say. I think I would have gone to my execution rather than admit to Dyson that I was neither mature nor experienced enough to decide my future.

My aunt and I were busy with preparations for the ball. Aunt Rose received letters from Courtney, and she read extracts to me; brief words of affection and re-assurance into which I read secret messages. He could not be more explicit. His mother was thoughtless, leaving such things about, and we could not risk the chance of any prying eyes. She must have realised what we were planning, even though she knew no details. Sometimes as we worked at our preparations for the ball together, she would forget and say things like 'when you two children are married . . .' or 'I had always imagined a great wedding here when Courtney married, all the county to attend . . .' and we would glance at each other then, nervously over our shoulders, smiling in secret understanding. Once again we were both waiting, but only I knew what for and when.

My dress was finished two days before the ball and I went in to Scarborough with Janet to collect it and several other items, dance-programmes and place-name cards, and the satin shoes which had been dyed a pale violet to match my gown.

It was a cold, blustery evening with a bad light and a threat of rain in the wind when we returned and Oldroyd brought the closed brougham to the station to meet us. As we jingled along the Grand Parade we passed two figures whom I recognised, Mrs. McAllister and little Andrew. Her frail figure was bent against the spatter of rain. In one hand she held a shopping basket, and by the other her little son, whose small legs were dragging wearily. As we passed she bent and picked Andrew up to carry him. It was nearly two miles to Ivy Lodge. Without a second thought I pulled the cord and Oldroyd brought the carriage to a stop.

I pulled down the glass and leaned out, waiting for them to come level with us. Mrs. McAllister might not want to know me but I could not let her walk all the way to Ivy Lodge with such a small child.

She stopped when I spoke to her, gazing at me with her great dark eyes, and when I suggested driving her home, hesitated, making me a little impatient.

'Mrs. McAllister, I am not in the habit of forcing my attentions on anyone. It is just that it is a long way to your home, and it begins to rain. Andrew is very small to walk so far, but I am sure, very heavy for you to carry. I assure you you will not be under any obligation to me.'

I opened the door and she got in, thanking me in a reserved way. Janet sat in her corner and stared in her country way at the thin, tired untidy woman, so shabby and fragile in her worn costume and unfashionable bonnet, and then at the small boy who said promptly, 'Why do you stare at me so?' which made her flush and glance away, but made me laugh.

'Is she an ayah or a *mem-sahib?*' he demanded.

'Janet is my maid, and my good friend,' I replied.

'What is in all these boxes?'

'They are new clothes.' I had bought a packet of Swiss chocolate, and I gave him one of the silver-wrapped discs, which he accepted graciously, and his small, delicate fingers unwrapped it with a curious unchildlike precision.

'Why do you need new clothes?' he demanded.

'In a few days it will be my birthday and my aunt is giving a ball for me.'

'My mama,' he said, 'never has new clothes and never goes to balls.'

Mrs. McAllister burst suddenly into a convulsive fit of weeping.

'Janet,' I said, 'have you my salts . . . here . . .' I moved beside Mrs. McAllister on the opposite seat, and proffered the smelling salts and a dry clean handkerchief. 'Take these, please don't be distressed.'

Andrew's eyes began to fill with tears, and Janet, evidently afraid that he too might start to weep, drew him on to her knee. 'Nay, then, don't thee start, love. It's wet enough outside by all accounts.'

Mrs. McAllister managed a faint smile, and I said consolingly, trying to make light of it and give her a chance of controlling her distress, 'Children say things they only half understand.'

'I do understand, madam lady,' Andrew said furiously. 'It is true. Ever since we have left Calcutta we have not enough money, and I like not this place where we have no servants but horrid old Janhoo and it is always cold.'

'Hush, darling,' said his mother. 'I am so sorry. I did not want to burden anyone with my worries. I have the expenses of the house and — and things are difficult — temporarily, I hope.'

'And the business you mentioned to me — your law case? That is not yet settled?'

She looked at me blankly for a moment, and then said, 'Oh, yes — the case. No. I am still waiting. It is very long, and my — my adviser is not here to help me.'

We turned into the drive of Ivy Lodge. It looked gloomy and cold, no flicker of firelight or gleam of illumination within. Janet said, 'I'll take t'little lad, madam.' She got out, lifted Andrew down and carried him through the now teeming rain to the porch. For a moment Mrs. McAllister and I were alone.

'Thank you,' she said. I guessed that she had not had the money to hire a hackney from the town. 'I was tired and we should have been very wet. It was kind of you.'

'It's nothing.'

The front door had opened, and I could see the Indian woman standing inside, holding a candle in her hand.

Mrs. McAllister suddenly put out her hand, and caught my wrist in a close fierce grip. 'My ayah has a little English, she gossips sometimes with local people — she says you are to be married to your cousin.'

'Then she knows more than I do!' I was annoyed. 'Nothing has been settled.'

'Then it is not true?'

'It is certainly not true that there has been any announcement.'

Her fingers relaxed, and I said sharply. 'Considering, Mrs. McAllister, that you discouraged my overtures of friendship you take a great deal of interest in my affairs.'

She sighed. 'I apologise. I am a woman alone with much to worry about, but not a great deal to occupy my time. I had hoped it was true ... I have been told Mr. Dyson Somerby is a fine man.'

His name caught me off guard. 'Mr. Dyson Somerby!' I exploded. 'My cousin Dyson is my guardian. That is all. He is the last man I would ever marry. It is my younger cousin, Courtney, with whom I have an understanding.'

She did not say anything. I had given myself away. Now it was my turn to plead.

'I should not have told you that. I was cross that you should think I would marry Dyson. Mrs. McAllister — there is no engagement, nothing of that sort between Courtney and myself, nothing *official*. Please don't suggest to anyone that there is. I am under age — it would be embarrassing to us all.'

'Yes ...' the word was breathed, a suspiration. 'Yes ... I see that it would be so.' She gave me a strange, wild look, and got down from the carriage and hurried into her uninviting house.

Janet got in and Oldroyd touched up the bay and at that moment I heard again the clicking sound, metallic and very faint — I could not be sure whether it was the harness jingling, or the anklets and bracelets of the ayah Janhoo standing half-hidden in the darkness of the hall. I gave a little shiver and Janet pulled the fur-lined rug up over our knees as we drove back to Sutherdyke.

'Aye, poor thing. I reckon brass is short in yon place. And that foreign woman wi' no more idea of making a Yorkshire house warm than I have o' flying! Bare legs, no petticoats, wrapped in an old shawl. No fire in t'hall. One candle. No coals in t'house, as like as not. Let's hope there's food for the bairn there.'

When I went into Sutherdyke out of the cold night a great fire was blazing in the open fireplace in the hall, and indeed in all the rooms we might occupy that night. Lamps and clusters of candles shone on the furniture and pictures — when the service door opened the faint smell of appetising cooking came momentarily from the kitchens. Aunt Bessy's bare cottage on The Quay at Monkstonby was cosier than Ivy Lodge.

Janet carried my shopping upstairs and I stood irresolutely in the hall, and then on an impulse I went to the door of the library and knocked. I had not done this for a long time. Not since Courtney's return. Before, if I had wanted anything, pocket money, a new dress, I would rush to Dyson, demanding, pleading, wheedling like the child I was then. But not any more. I waited until I heard him call for me to enter and was standing opposite him before he looked up from his work with an unguarded expression of pleasure which I could not believe. Immediately I imagined he was triumphant because I had come to him — but he need not think I had come for myself.

He leaned back in his chair and rubbed his long stubborn upper lip with his thumb and said, 'Well, what is it, Isabel? Are you planning to elope? I didn't think you would give me notice of that.'

My heart seemed to stop. For a moment I thought he knew, that by some kind of second-sight he had found out, then realised that he was teasing me.

'Don't be silly,' I said, but my cheeks were red, and I could see he was amused that I was disconcerted. He always made me feel like a kitten with its fur on end, small, furious and quite helpless.

'Well, what is it? I'm very busy. You don't often condescend to speak to me these days, so I'll spare you a few minutes.'

'Coming back from the station just now I picked up Mrs. McAllister from Ivy Lodge with her little boy. They were walking from Monkstonby station. From her manner and what she said they are in a hard way. I don't think she could afford a cab from the town ... she was distressed.'

He sat looking down at the papers on his desk, his strong hard face uncompromising.

'I know they are not our tenants – but it is my property. I wondered if you had heard anything about this ... there is a small boy ... they are gentlefolk ... I would not like to think ...' My voice died off on an ineffectual note of enquiry. Dyson sat back and looked at me.

'The leaseholder told me that she had not paid this month's rent if that is what you are wondering. She paid one month in advance, through the London agent. Nothing since. I have heard she owes money to tradesmen in Monkstonby. But then she is a stranger and a foreigner, and this would make them careful about credit.'

'You don't think her landlord will ...'

'Evict her?' He smiled unexpectedly and it was like a cloud-break over a bleak grey sea. 'It's unlikely.'

'Could you ask him to wait? I know you don't like doing these things, but perhaps — in this case?'

'Do you expect me to behave like the villain of the piece? Dogwhip and bloodhound? Simon Magree? Curled mostachois? Out into the storm, woman? You are a goose, Isabel.'

'I'm sorry.'

'In business one is only hard on those who can pay and won't. Not on the helpless.' He made a note on his pad. 'I'll make a few enquiries and see how things are with her.'

His kindness always disarmed me. It was not so easy to make him my enemy. I could fight him when he was harsh and overbearing. I began to move towards the door, thanking him as I did so, when he said, 'Isabel!' And I stopped and waited, and then to my utter astonishment, he said simply, 'I'm sorry. I'm sorry for what I did the other day.'

He rose to his great height and came to my side.

'Nay, don't be afraid,' he said. 'Don't look like that. I should not have done it. It was a terrible thing to do. I've no excuse, except that you've a lot of your mother in you — not just her grand looks. Sometimes you set out to drive people crazy, don't you Isabel?'

'Perhaps.'

'But you're a kind child for all your tantrums and romancing and wild ideas. One day, if you don't do anything daft — anything you'll regret, you may be a fine woman. Worthy to be rich. It's not easy to be worthy of fortune, you know.' He held out his hand to me, and without realising that I had moved, I put my hand into his and it disappeared into his grip. But it did not crush mine — it was light as a spaniel's mouth on a bird. He opened his fingers, looked at my hand for a moment, and then abruptly let it go.

'Right,' he said and went back to his desk. 'My mother says the plans for this dance of yours are going ahead. Have you heard from that brother of mine since we had that set-to here?'

'I haven't heard from him but my aunt has.'

'Yes,' he said briefly. 'She told me. I shall be relieved to see him here again, just to set her mind at rest. She worries when he is away — I understand that. He is a person to worry about.'

'Why? He's not a child.'

He looked at me, and then said, 'For many reasons. No doubt he will come back when he is short of cash.'

I turned away again, rather contemptuously.

'One cannot speak to you for five minutes without mentioning money. There are other things in life than money.'

'Aye, more's the pity. It would be a simple life if there

116

were not.' His voice and manner were still kindly, for although Dyson could lose his temper and flay with his tongue, although he could be harsh and stubborn when he believed himself right, he could never bear a grudge. 'You remember I said I would ask Mr. Shawcross to bring some of your mother's jewellery so you could choose a piece to wear at your ball? I have arranged it. He will bring you some pieces on the night.'

'Thank you.'

'Though you don't need jewels, Isabel. You'll be the brightest there, whatever you wear.'

There was no hint of irony — I realised with a shock that he admired me, that at least in some way my aunt was right. This great big dry-as-dust Yorkshire bear. I could have laughed. It gave me a sense of power. Or triumph. Knowing that I could hurt him as he hurt me. But I answered pertly, 'Perhaps you would like to put me up for a show prize, like one of your pedigree wool sheep, Cousin Dyson.'

His great roar of laughter filled the room, the first time I had heard him laugh since he and Courtney had quarrelled.

'You may be half Spanish but you've a true North-country tongue, Isabel. Be off with you now, and stop your sulking. Remember we're friends again.'

I was glad to let him think so. It was safer so. But he was still my enemy and now I knew I was not completely unarmed against him.

It was after five now and my aunt would have long since taken her tea. I went to the blue drawing-room to speak to her before going up to my room to change. She was not there but her escritoire was open with the gold-printed ball invitations and envelopes arranged in neat piles beside the guest list. I picked up her pen and impulsively wrote out an invitation to Mrs. McAllister, put it in

an envelope and addressed it to Ivy Lodge. I slipped it
into the pile ready to be despatched, wrote the name into
the guest list and ticked it as completed. At least, I
thought, the poor lady would realise I meant to be
friendly if she would permit me to do so. Courtney would
be angry — but he need not speak with her. But I
doubted, in any case, that she would come.

The day of my ball dawned at last, bringing my aunt a
letter from Courtney, saying he would be arriving that
evening, and containing a brief note for me. She gave it to
me when we were alone. It was the first word I had had
from him directly since he had quarrelled with Dyson. He
had arranged everything, he said. He would tell me everything when he saw me. I must be ready to leave at dawn. I
saw my aunt looking at me questioningly.

'Good news?'

'The best,' I said, and felt suddenly as though I was
standing again on the cliff-edge at Norhead and it was in
Courtney's power to destroy me if he wished. I was giving
my life into his keeping. I remembered the brilliant white
light of premonition telling me that whatever happened,
whatever he might do to others, he could never hurt me or
bring me to any harm and the memory of that moment
allayed my fears.

'Are you well, Isabel?' my aunt asked anxiously. 'You
are so white.'

'Yes.'

'It's tonight, isn't it?' she whispered, and when I
nodded her face filled with triumphant delight.

'At last,' she said, 'he will be happy as he deserves.' She
kissed me. 'You need not worry. I shall not say anything.
You have my blessing, Isabel.'

Mr. Shawcross and the Lister family had been invited
to dine with us before the ball.

The arrangements for our visit to London were fixed

for the New Year. They had many London friends and May chattered excitedly about the balls we should go to, the invitations, the excursions, theatres, the opera — but most of all the exciting young men we should meet.

I listened silently. By tomorrow I would be sailing with Courtney for Scotland. By the New Year I should be his wife. How and in what circumstances should we be living? He loved me. I should be safe with him. He could never harm me. When we were married, what could Dyson do? Nothing. We should return here to Sutherdyke, married lovers, and be happy together.

But my nerves were a jangle of excitement. I had packed a small valise and hidden it in my wardrobe. I had put travelling clothes ready, and all the money I had in my handbag. I wished I could take Janet with me, and thought I would ask Courtney if I could. When she helped me dress that night I cried, and then laughed, and clung to her as I used to as a baby, and she stroked my hair, and comforted me, wondering if I had a fever, or if it was just excitement, telling me 'not to take on so' and giving me sal volatile to calm my nerves.

My gown was made from the violet and silver sari that Courtney had brought me back from India, draped over a stiff white satin. Janet dressed my hair in a high chignon with small white and purple orchids, like a small coronet of flowers.

Just before dinner Dyson sent for me and I found him in the small library with Mr. Shawcross and my aunt. On the desk were the leather jewellery boxes which the solicitor had brought, all open, their contents gleaming on their velvet beds.

The brilliance took my breath away, but to my surprise did not give me the delight I had anticipated. I stood silently looking down at them, and Dyson came to my side.

'Disappointed, Isabel? Are they not as bonny as you hoped?'

'They are more beautiful than I dreamed. It is sad he gave her all these yet could not make her happy.'

There was one pair of earrings with no stones, simple rings such as gypsies wear, but of chased gold. In the lid of the box there was the name of a jeweller in Madrid.

'These came from Spain,' I said.

My aunt glanced at them indifferently. 'Then my brother could not have bought them for her. He met her in Paris, and he was never with her in Spain.'

'Perhaps she bought them for herself,' I said. 'I'll wear them.' I fastened them in my ears, and through the mirror saw them all looking at me. 'The dancer's earrings for the dancer's daughter,' I said.

My aunt looked affronted, but Dyson selected another jewel, a brooch of amethysts and emeralds and diamonds, fashioned like a bunch of violets. 'Wear this too, Isabel,' he said. 'It's a pretty thing and goes with your gown. You may be the dancer's daughter, but you are also the heiress of Sutherdyke.'

But I did not want to be reminded of that tonight. I did not want to think of duty or responsibility. I only wanted to think of Courtney. I silently pinned the violet brooch on my dress, sick with impatience for his coming. The guests for the ball would be arriving at nine. Dinner time arrived and he still had not come. It was obvious that my aunt too was watching the clock, glancing furtively at me as she made conversation with Mrs. Lister.

I went in to dinner with Mr. Shawcross. He had always known the family and had known my mother.

'I was the only man your father would trust her with — I suppose because I was such a dull sort of chap.' He sounded rather wistful, as though her remembered beauty made him wish to have been a little more dashing. He told me about the jewels.

'After her death everything was kept there as though she was coming back at any time. Sir Lockwood said she was dancing a European tour, but she would come back. He would never go to her grave, or admit she was dead. He had always been afraid that something or someone would take her away from him.'

'Something or someone? What do you mean?'

He hesitated, and I realised that even though her marriage had now been established she was not the sort of woman an elderly gentleman discusses with a young girl. I put my arm in his and smiled into his eyes. 'Please? I am not ashamed of her.'

He patted my hand, shaking his head. 'Perhaps if your family, your grandmother and Mrs. Somerby had not been, things would have been better. She was a glorious creature, but every breath she drew made him jealous, she longed for the old life, the adulation, the fame, her career, but it was sickness and a baby that took her from him in the end.'

'Did she ever wear the jewels?'

'Perhaps before she came to Sutherdyke — mostly she wore those earrings you are wearing tonight.' He looked at me for a long moment and then said, 'You are extraordinarily like her. The jewel cases were found in her room after Sir Lockwood's death and in one of them was her marriage certificate and your birth certificate. It was after that Dyson brought you to live at Sutherdyke.'

'But — he could have destroyed the documents,' I said, 'and left me at Monkstonby.'

'So he could, my dear, and it's doubtful whether anyone would have discovered it. But that's not Dyson's way.' Mr. Shawcross beamed across the flowers and glass of the table at the subject of this conversation, who was eating his entrée and listening patiently to May Lister's chatterings. 'That's not the Somerby way,' said Mr. Shawcross. 'When Dyson and Courtney were little boys, all their father's money went to his creditors — payment in full. There were many who would have lent him money to start again, if he had lived. The Somerbys were not gentry — they were West Riding weavers, but they were good, proud folk, and honest.'

'And the Broadbents are aristocrats but bad folk?'

He laughed and shook his head. 'You don't catch me out like that, Miss Broadbent. There is bad and good in all families. But I've always found it strange that Dyson there seems to be all Somerby, while Courtney is a Broadbent all through.'

'But if you had to do business, you would prefer to do it with the Somerbys?'

'The Broadbents do no business, they do not need to. They are very rich. But where is Courtney?'

'He is coming tonight,' I said hurriedly. 'He has been away in London.'

'He was always away to London, even when he was a boy,' said Mr. Shawcross, and I heard the doubt in his voice.

At nine I took my stand by my aunt's side to welcome the guests. I saw a little snow of white and violet on the floor and found I was nervously picking the orchids in my bouquet. Every time the door opened our hearts rose in anticipation, and fell with a disappointment we concealed behind conventional words of greeting.

'Surely nothing could have happened to Courtney,' my aunt whispered. 'Tonight of all nights. He would have let us know if anything had happened to prevent him coming.'

'Remember when he came from India, how we waited without a word from him. He will come in his own good time, and it will be all right. You'll see.'

But I was far from being as confident as I sounded. I was full of unacknowledged fears. But I held my head high, smiled and murmured polite, affectionate or respectful greetings to my guests as they crossed the outer hall to where I stood with my aunt and Dyson.

We stood there for an hour receiving. Here were all the important families in the Riding attending my ball and acknowledging me as my father's legitimate daughter. Sir Hugo Transome, the Lord Lieutenant, and his wife were bringing their daughter who had been at school with me in Scarborough. I should have been very proud, and I suppose in a way I was as I stood bowing and smiling, automatically extending my white gloved hand, speaking the set phrases of welcome. But all the time I was watching the door for Courtney's slender, bright-haired figure. Every time Hawkins opened it I thought that surely, *surely* this time he would appear. But time went by, the steady stream of guests dwindled and then ceased and he had not come. I glanced at my aunt and knew that she too was unbearably anxious and beneath her rouge her handsome face was white with strain. We exchanged uncertain smiles of comfort, whispered to each other that he was never on time, that he would come when we least expected and when it suited him.

'That seems to be the last,' said Dyson in relief. 'There is no need for you to stand there any longer, Isabel. Go into your guests now and dance and enjoy yourself.' He glanced from his mother to me, a slow searching glance that seemed to know my secrets, so I went at once towards the great hall where a waltz was being played and the dancing was in fullswing.

Dyson knew Courtney was coming and I did not want him to know anything further. I did not want my anxiety to betray me.

I heard the door open again and Hawkins announce

another guest and turned back again eagerly. Mrs. McAllister stood framed against the arched doorway clutching a Kashmir shawl about her thin shoulders. I had forgotten my impulsive invitation to her. I saw my aunt's startled face and with a murmured explanation advanced, holding out my hand in greeting.

She was wearing a ball gown of ivory and gold brocade, crumpled, as though it had been taken from a trunk without any kind of freshening. She looked as though she had decided to come at the last moment without thought for her appearance. I could see she was not wearing evening shoes but outdoor shoes of leather, coated with gravel and mud, and her long black hair, as vaguely secured as ever, was wet with rain and lying smoothly against her delicate head, making her look startling Oriental. It was quite obvious that she had walked the mile or more from Ivy Lodge.

My aunt extended distant finger tips and turned away.

'Mrs. McAllister,' I said, 'I am so glad you decided to come.' I was aware of Dyson, just behind me, silently watching.

'I shouldn't have come perhaps, I was not prepared, but I must talk with you, Miss Broadbent.'

I was terrified. I knew her presence near Sutherdyke was not mere chance, and that I had really known it from the moment I had taken little Andrew in my arms and ridden home with him on my saddle. I knew that this woman was connected in some way with Courtney's life in India and that tonight she had come to tell me what it was — I knew too, that I did not want to hear. I was afraid of knowing. I had planned everything. I had shut my ears and eyes and refused to listen to anything which might destroy my happiness. I would not listen now. I was too near to everything I had longed for; it was in my grasp after all these long years and I could not let go.

I looked wildly around and saw our most important

guest and his wife smiling at me from the door of the great hall, the coloured dresses of the dancers swinging past behind them. I smiled and waved, turned back to Mrs. McAllister, speaking in a cool society voice, a little distant, as though I would not admit any intimacy although mildly glad that she had come.

'Of course I would like to talk with you, Mrs. McAllister, but not at the moment. I have only greeted my guests and I must go to the ballroom. Sir Hugo and his wife are waiting for me ... I must not keep the Lord Lieutenant waiting ...'

'But, Miss Broadbent, I must speak to you. I have been told that you ...'

'No!' I said almost savagely, all my inherited Broadbent tenacity rejecting her, refusing to listen. 'I cannot now ...'

She changed colour and swayed and Dyson, who had neither moved nor spoken, went to her side and supported her, his big hand holding her thin arm.

'But you are not well,' I cried.

'I am tired — I have been anxious ... I have no carriage so I had to walk ...'

'Then you must rest and have some refreshment, and get warm. Dyson, will you look after Mrs. McAllister, please, while I go and speak to my other guests? ...'

She recovered herself with an effort and began to plead with me to stay, but I shook my head, smiled my charming, artificial social smile. Later, I said, of course, later in the evening I would have time for a chat. But I had no intention of seeking her out or finding the time. I touched Dyson's arm gratefully as I skimmed by, my skirts rustling behind me, and went straight to the Lord Lieutenant.

'Sir Hugo — are you looking for me? I am so sorry to have kept you ... and how charming of you to wait. Yes, I will have my very first dance with you ...'

The old soldier swept me into the dancers in perfect time, pivoting smoothly on his ramrod spine, feeling, poor pet, twenty years younger because I had honoured him. Over his shoulder I saw Mrs. McAllister watching us, distraught and exhausted, and I saw Dyson lead her away to a seat at the far end of the hall in the recess of one of the great oriel windows and offer her a glass of champagne. She took it helplessly, sipped it, and then sat with the glass in her hands, watching me move among the dancers. She looked strange and fragile beside Dyson's great height — like a ghost, a *revenante* — a returned one — eerie among the well-dressed, well-groomed youngsters swinging past her. I saw that Dyson had taken a seat beside her, and that suddenly she was talking to him with a passionate intensity while he sat listening, his eyes and face still and expressionless as stone. Every now and then her spate of words would falter, and she would look desperately about the room and I knew, like me, she was waiting for Courtney and the thing she wanted to tell me was about him and I did not want to hear.

My ball was, in a way, a country dance, not too stiff and formal, my guests were friends and county neighbours and many of the girls I had been to school with were there. If the majority of the guests were rich, they were simple people too, able to enjoy themselves heartily. Among the waltzes were many country dances, Sir Roger de Coverley, and a racing gallop to John Peel with the wild call of hunting horns echoing under the cross-beams of the roof. My aunt said it was like old times — when she and my father were young. I drank three glasses of champagne, I laughed and danced and flirted and pretended to be happy, and that the hours were flying past instead of dragging minute by heavy minute because Courtney was not there.

It was just before midnight — the supper was to be

served in the dining-room and the blue drawing-room. May and some of my school friends surrounded me, pleading with me to dance for the company.

In the past summers I had often danced at fêtes and garden parties, but I had not intended to dance tonight. I knew my aunt would not like it, but now, as the girls importuned me, I suddenly agreed. I sent for my mother's castanets and told the orchestra to play a Spanish tune. I wanted to remind my aunt and everyone else of my mother, Maria-Amata, the girl whom none of them had condescended to know. She was the reason for the ball, for my being there, for everything that had happened. I wanted to show everyone that I was as proud of her as I was of being a Broadbent and heiress to Sutherdyke. I wanted to show the Somerbys, for it was they who had wanted to forget her, and in some illogical way I was dancing for Courtney too, hoping that he would come and see me and want me more than ever.

My little dance which I had learned at school had nothing of the savage intensity of the real flamenco. But I had read about it, and seen the faded photographs of my mother. I could make the castanets ripple and rattle and bend my body in the fine gypsy arch, walk with the proud strut and high head of the Spanish dancers and stamp out the cross rhythms with my heels. I had made it quite a different thing, wilder and more seductive, than the innocuous little routine we had learned at dancing class.

I saw Dyson watching me. He had never seen me dance before and his face was strange, remote and sad and when I smiled at him he turned away. And then — at last I saw Courtney. I had not seen him enter the room, but suddenly he was there, standing in the doorway with his mother, watching me. She looked happy and relaxed because he had arrived and was with her, but she watched me with unguarded dislike and disgust. I was too like the woman who had taken so much from her — all her expectations and high ambitions. I remember Dyson saying 'You think of her as an ally. I tell you she thinks of nothing but your fortune for her lovely boy,' and I knew it was true. If I had been poor she would not have even pretended an affection for me.

But Courtney's eyes were brilliant. His cheeks were flushed, a lock of hair fell across his forehead, so like the wilful boy I had fallen in love with six years ago. I knew that both the Somerby brothers were watching me, and I could go to either as I wished. Which road should I follow — Dyson's, slow, sober and responsible, or Courtney's path of passionate and reckless love? But when I met Courtney's eyes and saw the adoration in them I knew that whatever else was evasive and even false in his nature, this at least, his passion for me, was deeply felt and passionately true — then I knew which way I wanted to go.

I finished my dance to a burst of applause, and refusing all their demands for an encore, ran across to Courtney.

'You are so late,' I cried, 'I have been waiting and waiting. I thought you were not coming.'

'I've had so much to arrange,' he said softly. I was wild with excitement. The orchestra broke into a Strauss waltz and people took their partners for the supper dance. Courtney put his arm about me and swung me unresistingly into the stream of dancers and for the first time that evening I was happy. He put his lips against my ear, speaking softly.

'Isabel, are you ready to come with me tonight?'

'I have been ready for days. I have been frantic with fear. I thought something had happened — an accident or something terrible to prevent your coming.'

'There were last-minute things to arrange. A carriage to wait for us outside away from the house. I had to find someone whom I could trust not to gossip. We will take the carriage to Driffield and then get an early train from there. We would be recognised at Monkstonby. Tell Janet not to wake you early and then they will think you are sleeping late after the ball. I have everything arranged. Money, our passages in the steamer, lodgings reserved in Aberdeen. We will stay there quiet and concealed until we can be married, and then . . .'

'Then we will come back here and tell Dyson, and he will have to accept it, and then . . .'

He stumbled a little and changed colour. I followed his glance to where Mrs. McAllister was seated in the deep bay looking at us. She had a greenish pallor and her great eyes burned. She looked as though she would faint.

'What is that woman doing here?'

'I asked her to come. She is harmless enough and seems friendless — what does it matter?'

His arm dropped from about me. He walked through the dancers towards her, leaving me standing there alone. He seemed possessed by some inner, burning fury. I had never seen him look like this. The cliché 'if looks could kill' was true. *He was wishing her dead.*

He stopped before her, spoke briefly and offered her his arm. She rose, swaying, her face drawn and terrible, and went with him out into the hall. I hoped that no one had noticed, but Mr. Shawcross and Sir Hugo, chatting together at the edge of the circling dancers, looked astounded and affronted, old beaux that they were. I went to them at once, saying quickly, 'My neighbour Mrs. McAllister is not well. I have sent Courtney to take her somewhere cooler to recover. If you will excuse me I will go and see how she is.'

To my relief they seemed to accept this explanation, and I hurried into the hall. If I was missed during supper it would certainly cause comment. There was no sign of

Courtney and Mrs. McAllister in the outer hall — it was full of hired waiters carrying food and wine into the supper rooms under the direction of their *maître d'hôtel* who seemed to be carrying on some kind of guerrilla warfare with Hawkins, who felt himself usurped. Their voices, raised in disagreement over the temperature of wine, dropped as I entered, and to my question, Hawkins said he had seen Mr. Courtney take the foreign lady along to the winter-garden.

I went down the west corridor to the morning-room door. It was closed but beyond it I could hear Courtney's voice raised in passion, the furious anger that I had so often heard in the library during his interminable arguments with Dyson about money. I stood looking at the polished oaken panels and the ornately worked brass handle, not wanting to open the door just as I had not wanted to listen to Elspeth McAllister earlier in the evening. Then I slowly put out my hand and turned the knob and opened the door.

There was only a low lamp burning in the morning-room. The french windows leading into the winter-garden were open and it was lit with small coloured Chinese lanterns hung among the foliage so that sentimental couples could linger between dances among the ferns and vines.

Courtney was standing there and Elspeth McAllister was on her knees at his feet, clinging to him, her whole body shaken with passionate weeping. As I stood there he raised his arm as though to strike her and I cried out in protest, so that he looked at me, a terrible look, the look of one in despair.

He lifted her to her feet, put her shawl about her shoulders, opened the door into the garden and seemed to thrust her outside. I ran forward and would have followed, but he barred my way.

'How dare she come here?' he cried.

'I told you — I asked her to come. Let me go.'

'I will not permit you to speak to such a creature.'

'Courtney, let me go to that poor woman or I will fetch Dyson and rouse the house.'

'I will not!' I made a move to run back into the hall, but he caught my wrist. 'I will not let you follow her. Let her go back to the gutter she came from. She is not fit to be in the same room as you.'

'What is she to you? Did she follow you from India?'

His face filled with an unbearable pain.

'Isabel, you must try to understand and forgive me. That time is past. You said yourself that it did not matter to you.'

'I thought then it did not matter. I don't want to sit in judgment on your past. But I must know. Mrs. McAllister is in great distress and she seems a person of refinement.' He made a fierce, scornful exclamation, and I asked the question that had been haunting me all evening. 'Is the child yours?'

'The child?'

'There is a little boy.'

'How should I know whom the brat belongs to? I doubt if she does herself! I told you I had not lived like a monk. She was my mistress. I put her out of my life when I sailed for home and she followed me here to blackmail me. The daughter of a Scottish engineer and a native woman, a bazaar woman. She is one of these creatures on the fringe of Anglo-Indian society. She has no claim on me. I told her this before I left India.'

I was shattered — not because he had a mistress, but because of his cruelty.

'If she were a street-walker,' I stormed, 'she would deserve some consideration. Suppose I go with you tonight, would you throw me aside when you are bored or some-one more attractive appeared?'

'Isabel, you are my love, my only real love and I want you for my wife. There is no comparison.'

'I think there is a very good comparison. The daughter of a Scottish engineer and a native woman. What am I but the daughter of a profligate baronet and a gypsy dancer? You make fine distinctions, Courtney. Perhaps there is only one. That I am rich.'

His face went white. His arm dropped and he turned away. I thrust open the door and went out into the cold darkness. It was still outside, but a fine snow was be-ginning to fall and the air struck icily on my hot cheeks and bare shoulders. The damp grass soaked my satin shoes. I called her name — I ran about the garden, along the lawn, into the rose-garden, the snowflakes falling on my lips and hair, chill and wet. Everything was still and no one answered. It was silent with the winter silence of the countryside — silent, until at my elbow almost, I heard the little clattering-chinking sound of the rose-garden ghost and cried out with fear as I saw Janhoo standing near me in the shadow of the yew hedge. I heard Courtney call me, and heard his footsteps as he searched for me, and turned to the little woman who stood wrapped in her grey woollen shawl, her withered brown face hidden in the white cotton veil she always wore draped about her head.

'Janhoo, thank God you are here. Where is your mis-tress? Where is Mrs. McAllister?'

'The *mem-sahib*?' She pointed to the house, and the thin bracelets chinked on her brown twig of an arm.

'No, the *mem-sahib* has gone. She is very distressed. She is ill. Find her and care for her, Janhoo, and tell her that tomorrow I will come and talk with her. I must go. Find her, please, Janhoo!'

I ran back to the winter-garden, lifting my trailing
skirts from the settling snow, meeting Courtney on the
gravel path outside. He put his arms about me and drew
me inside.

'You are shivering. It is bitter outside ... you mad
child, you'll be ill.' I was stony and withdrawn. His touch
could still move me, but I did not want it. He began to
speak with agonising sincerity.

'Isabel, you must hear me. I had not planned to love
you. I knew I was not fit to love you. I fought against it
when I first returned, you know that I did. But God help
me, I do love you. If you hadn't a penny in the world it
would be just the same.'

He seemed to be clinging to me in his need and despair,
as my father had clung to Maria-Amata.

'I have been mad and bad, I know, and perhaps I am
all the things which Dyson thinks I am. But I love you,
Isabel. No one will ever love you as I do.' I shivered, but
he went on, 'I know that with you my whole world will be
different. I shall be different. Don't be afraid to trust
yourself to me. I would never hurt you or let anything
hurt you. I swear we shall be happy as we were in the old,
innocent days, when you were barely out of childhood.
Don't turn me away. I cannot imagine life without you.
You have become my reason for life.'

It was as though my father, Sir Lockwood, was alive
again, wandering through the great house in search of his
dead love. The intensity, the desperation, the single purpose.

'I can't hold you to your promise,' he said. 'You have
waited for me in the past. Now I will wait for you. I will
wait for you in the carriage. I have ordered to stand fifty
yards from the main gates after the last guests have gone. I
will wait for you to come to me, and if you don't come,
you will never see me again.'

'Courtney . . . don't speak so wildly . . .' I began, but he would not listen. He stood there thin and tense, with the blue eyes blazing at me, so that it seemed he would flame and disintegrate with the intensity of his passion.

'I'm past everything. It is you or nothing. I will wait for you, and if you do not come by dawn, I shall know you will not come, and I shall know what to do.'

Without another word he left me, and a few minutes later he left the house.

I did not know what to do. The ball seemed endless. I avoided my aunt, whose joy and triumph vanished when I went into the supper room without Courtney. I talked, I laughed. Dyson gravely proposed my health. I thanked my guests for their good wishes and presence there. I felt like a puppet whose lips and movements are being moved by strings. I do not know what I said, what I laughed at, whom I danced with. Afterwards I was told that I had never appeared more brilliant or beautiful.

It was four o'clock when the last guests left — they drove away into a night of snow and bitter cold, huddling under the carriage rugs.

Hawkins and the tired servants went round extinguishing the lights and clearing away the remains of food and wine until Dyson bade them leave it until morning and get off to their beds.

He stopped me as I went upstairs.

'You haven't been happy,' he said. 'Have you?'

'No.'

'I won't ask why. I wanted it to be your happiest day. Never mind. There will be other days — you have all your youth yet. Good night, Isabel.'

Youth? I felt old, dried-up, finished. What was I to do? What did Courtney mean? Was he threatening to take his life? I had sent Janet to bed — I had not wanted her there when I made my escape at dawn, but I had scarcely taken

134

off my ball gown when my aunt came in demanding to know where Courtney had gone and why. Had we quarrelled? What had happened?

I was too weary to deceive her any longer. I told her what had happened and what he had told me. She did not care. It meant nothing to her. I was a fool to expect anything else.

'When you are married you can pay the woman off. I know her sort — you will never hear of her again. What a milk-and-water fool you are, Isabel, to let such a thing come between you. You will not refuse him now. You will go? If you don't I shall never forgive you.'

'If I don't,' I said, 'what will he do?'

'If he said he will kill himself he will,' she said. 'I know. Once as a small boy when my husband stopped him getting his way he jumped from the roof. He was on his back for weeks. If he said he would do it he will. I cannot understand you. There is barely a man who has not a mistress somewhere.'

'It is not that,' I said — and it was not. It was his merciless rejection of Elspeth McAllister that I could not bear. It was his possessive passion for me that repulsed and frightened me. I remembered the old mad man, grasping at my skirts, calling me by Mother's name and my panic desire to escape. I had seen him look at me from Courtney's eyes that night. I had longed to be loved — I had never thought of being possessed.

'I'll go to meet him,' I said, 'but I won't go away with him. I will go and ask him to see reason and to wait for a while. I must have time to think.'

'He loves you. Isn't that enough?' she said fiercely. 'Do you want to destroy him now?'

I did not answer, and she left me alone. I took the flowers from my hair, put aside my gypsy earrings and glittering brooch, put on a thick dress and boots and my thick hooded cloak. I did not take my money, or my packed bag. I would go out and find Courtney and speak to him. I would tell him I could not leave with him now, but perhaps later, I might think differently ... I might find my love strong enough to forget what he had told me. Because I loved him still for all his terrible faults, and it was like an ache within me. And then, I thought that, after all, he might be right. If we went we would have each other, we would be together in our passionate love, and perhaps as he said we could build a new life from it. I went down the stairs and quietly through the silent house.

The key and the bolts slid easily, and I opened the door and stood hesitating in the cold. The sleet, lit by a clouded moon, fell blindingly outside.

A light fell across me from the hall, and Dyson stood there holding a lamp, enormously tall in his long belted gown.

We stood and looked at each other and to my astonishment there was no anger in his face, only pity, and he said, 'You must not go to him, Isabel.'

'I have to. I don't know what he will do.'

'Let him — for once let someone refuse him. I tell you, there are reasons why you cannot go. I do not want to stop you, but I will. I will hold you, whatever you do or say. I am not going to let him ruin your life as he has ruined his own and others'.'

The wind from the cold garden crept into the hall. I heard a sound — a faint, rattling metallic sound and turned sharply peering into the snow. I saw a figure, two figures dragging towards us, and as they came nearer I saw that one was the little gnarled Indian woman, Janhoo, her bracelets and anklets faintly clinking and she was half-dragging, half-supporting her mistress, whose hair was about her face, whose face streamed with blood, who although she stumbled slowly towards the light looked as though she was dead.

Dyson put down the lamp, plunged out into the snow and lifted her in his arms, carrying her into the house. The little Indian woman followed, chattering like a monkey, looking at me with eyes full of hate.

Dyson took Elspeth McAllister into the library, telling me to get water, towels and brandy, and when I came back he had loosened her cloak and she lay motionless on the settee.

'We must send for the doctor,' he said, but her eyes opened, and she caught his arm.

'No, *no*! No one else. No one must know.' She was barely audible — she seemed only half-conscious.

'Very well . . .' He seemed afraid she would die there and then. He rubbed her hands, told me to call Janet, get hot bricks, warm a bed, began to bathe the terrible contusions on her head and shoulders.

'Has she had an accident?' I asked fearfully.

He looked up at me.

'Her servant say he tried to kill her. He drove the horse at her when he saw her struggling alone along the road to Ivy Lodge.'

I still did not understand.

'Courtney,' he said bluntly, and the horror became clear.

'But why? Why should he do such a thing?'

'She is his wife.'

'Oh . . .' I reeled and caught a chair.

'Don't faint now, Isabel,' he said. 'Don't grieve. There will be time for both. Go and do as I told you. We must help her. No one else can.'

I dragged myself erect. I was beyond tiredness. I thought I might vomit. I poured some brandy, drank it neat, and forced myself to go and do his bidding.

CHAPTER SIX

I did not waken until late the following day. Dyson sent me to bed with a draught that put me asleep for ten hours without moving and when I woke I tried to hold on to sleep and stave off the memory of what had happened and what I had to face. It was late afternoon and Janet brought me a light meal on a tray which I made a pretence of eating. There would be no dinner served in the dining-room tonight, she said. My aunt was confined to her room, but Mr. Somerby would like me to come down when I felt rested enough. I knew I would never feel rested enough to hear what he had to say.

She told me that Mrs. McAllister had been put into one of the spare rooms, and that Mrs. Oldroyd had been driven over to Ivy Lodge to bring little Andrew back to her cottage to be cared for until his mother was strong enough to return home. Janet did not mention Courtney. I wondered if he had waited for me in that bleak dawn and where he was now. I did not wonder if he was dead. It would have been easier if he had been, I think, for then I could have forgiven him — or tried to. I began to weep weighted down by horror, loss and heartbreak. I cried for a long time and after a while Janet came and sat beside me and rocked me in her kind, strong arms as she had when we were children together.

Presently I recovered sufficiently to wash and dress, compose myself and go down to Dyson in the library. It was a curious meeting.

'Do you feel better, Isabel?'

'Yes.'

'And — strong?' I did not reply. 'Do you want to know it all? It's not a pretty story.'

'When did you first know?'

'Last night. She told me before he sent her away. She was very much afraid of something — I realised that some time ago, and guessed there was some connection between her and Courtney. I am suspicious and watchful by nature, and the coincidence of her arrival and Indian background suggested it.'

'I never dreamed of it — until last night.' I met his grave eyes and knew this was not true. I had been afraid. I had not wanted to know.

'But you did not want to believe anything of him but good.'

'How did you know we had planned to run away together?'

'I knew he had not come back for nothing and I was watching. I would not have let you go, Isabel, knowing what I did about him even before this poor woman told me who she was.'

'What did you know?'

'About his gambling and drinking, his women — and lately his drug-taking.'

'Whey did you not tell me?'

'Would you have believed me?' I tried to meet the hard question in his eyes and could not. 'You believed my mother who told you I was trying to destroy him so I could get you and your fortune for myself.' He rose, and said, 'Will you come and hear what Elspeth Somerby has to tell you? She is better, but still weak. I think it is better that she should tell you herself.'

So I went with him upstairs into a guest room where Elspeth lay. McAllister was her maiden name, the daughter, as Courtney had said, of a Scottish engineer. But not of a bazaar girl — of an Indian lady of good family. She had been an orphan, living quietly with a chaperon in a good part of Calcutta when Courtney first came into her life.

As I went into the semi-darkened room my aunt followed us. She seemed to have aged overnight and she wore black as though in mourning. She sat in a chair by the fireplace turned away from the bed, and I do not think she looked at Elspeth once during the whole time that we were in the room. I took a chair and Dyson stood back in the shadows by the bed curtains, a large and curiously sustaining presence. If the world were mad he stood for sanity.

Elspeth lay with her bandaged head propped on the pillows, her long black hair plaited over her shoulder. She was wearing one of my gowns. Her thin hands were folded on her breast and when she spoke her great, shadowed eyes looked round at us apologetically, almost as though the appalling story was her fault and not Courtney's, and she was to blame for our present unhappiness. The Indian servant, Janhoo, sat cross-legged by the bed, screwing up her baleful old face as she tried to follow what her mistress said, rocking and muttering to herself, watching us with her mad black eyes.

Elspeth's faint voice, with its slightly sing-song accent, told us how she had met Courtney in India. He had heard of her and deliberately sought her out. How she had fallen in love with him, had married him and how, when he had gone through her quite considerable fortune, he had deserted her and her boy. Sometimes her voice was so faint I looked at her in alarm, she sounded as though her life could not carry her sorrow any more. He was her first and only suitor, for even with money, suspended between two worlds by her mixed blood, marriage was not easy for her.

But he courted her ardently. She had no relatives on her father's side and Courtney insisted that she cut herself off completely from her mother's people. They were married secretly in Calcutta four years previously and she had a brief, illusive happiness and then he destroyed everything and nearly destroyed her. Bit by bit every scrap of joy, trust, peace of mind, security from want and even self respect, for she was ashamed of her terror of him — everything was whittled away, leaving nothing but her desperate and loyal love.

'And even if I had not loved him he was all I had left in the world. He never told anyone we were married. He would come to my house secretly after dark. He said it would ruin his army career if it were discovered. At first he said it must be kept secret just for a while, until his time in India was finished, but then later, he did not even pretend. When Andrew was born I did not see him for weeks, and he would never even look at him. He came less and less, and I had to accept that he had no intention of acknowledging us, that he was ashamed of us, that he had only wanted my money — and when he knew that I understood this he became very cruel and I became afraid. He would threaten to kill me — but for Andrew I would have been glad to die.' Her voice petered out, and I rose in alarm, but she said, 'Janhoo . . .' and stretched out her hand. The Indian woman fiercely clutched the weak hand in her brown claw, gazing round like a tiger as though daring us to touch her.

Elspeth smiled faintly as though the touch comforted her.

'I discovered, or Janhoo discovered, through the grape vine of news that runs round the bazaars, that he was planning to leave India without letting me know. By then all my money had gone. He had entertained at the station and in the mess, he had gambled, bought expensive horses, backed them, sold them for a loss. He was being dunned by tradesmen, money-lenders and bookmakers. He began to drink, to go to the streets where the bad houses are and where he learned to smoke opium.'

My aunt, her face averted, as though she could not bear the sight of the woman in the bed, said suddenly in a loud, unnatural voice, 'It is not true! She is lying. He was always a good boy. A beautiful, charming boy.'

Dyson made to put his arm about her but she shook him off. She could never bear him to touch her.

'It is true, Mother. Where do you think he was on those long unexplained absences?'

'He always amused himself, sometimes in low company, even as a boy. But he is a man. A true Broadbent like my brother, one expects this.'

'Mother,' Dyson said patiently, 'I learned of his addiction shortly after he arrived. You could smell the stuff on him when he came back from The Crown, sweet, heavy, sickly. That was why we quarrelled that night. I absolutely forbade him to involve Isobel in any way. I told him if he persisted I would tell her, and turn him out. So he went off again to The Crown, where the landlord kept a room for him and no questions asked. Or to Hull to the lascar houses by the docks.'

'Why did you not tell me? I might have helped him.'

'You have never helped him, Mother. You have only indulged him. He would have told you lies, as he always has. You would never have believed anything against him.'

I remembered the heavy sickly perfume, which I had thought was from the flowers in the winter-garden. We had been so eager to be deceived — my aunt and I.

'I sold up my house and raised enough money to follow him to England,' said Elspeth. 'When I confronted him in London I thought he would kill me then. Then he insisted

I take a house near Sutherdyke. He wanted me near, he said. He did not trust me far away from him. He gave me the money for the first month's rent, and I took Ivy Lodge. I had no choice — I was almost destitute and mad with worry. I was to make no acquaintances, go under my maiden name, keep to myself. At first he came — secretly by night, as he had in India. He told me that he was expecting the family to make a settlement on him, but that they would never accept me and Andrew. If they discovered who I was it would be the end of every hope of aid. I was too frightened to do anything else. He told me that Miss Broadbent was unattractive, plain and old, but she liked him and hoped to marry him, but he had no intention of marrying her — he was hoping she would marry his brother, and if she did she would settle some money on him and his mother ... a woman like that would be lucky to make any sort of match, he said. And then one day this beautiful girl rode up to my door with Andrew and I knew it was all lies again. But then I did not know the full horror of what was happening. That I did not know until last night, just before your ball, when Janhoo told me the truth.'

She was silent for a while, then said desperately, 'I have to tell you. I wish you did not care for him or that his mother love him so. It would be easier to tell. Janhoo is devoted to me. My father took her off the streets as a child. She is not quite normal. She comes from a criminal race, and knows how to bring about death. He told her that if you died, Miss Broadbent, that all my troubles would be over. He told her to kill you. I wondered why she would steal out in the dusk each evening. She followed you, watching for a chance to do you some secret mischief.'

I remembered the ghostly castanets, the faint clicking, chinking sound, the sense of being watched, the vague white figure watching through the glass of the winter-garden, and shuddered.

'But then she discovered that he no longer desired your death. He loved you. He told her he had new plans and she was not to go near you. He threatened to harm Andrew and me if she did not obey. You see he had forgotten you, what you were like. He had only thought of the money. He found you young and very lovely and ready to care for him too, and I really think for the first time in his life he was truly in love. I think he tried to go away from you, as sometimes he tried to keep away from his drugs, but he had not the strength. You see he lived in dreams and recently I do not think he could escape from them. He always believed that the miracle would happen, that people in his way would die, that fortune would come from the skies ... But these things do not happen. Our burdens stay with us. Poor Courtney!'

The tears ran down her thin face and Janhoo muttered to herself. I knew it was true. In some mad mistaken way he *had* loved me. I had known he could hurt others but not me. But I had not dreamed how he could hurt them and to what lengths he would go.

'It was not until the night of the ball she told me and by then I was beyond caring what happened to my life. I had not heard from him for weeks. I had no money, there was neither food nor fuel in the house, and your invitation came like some terrible mockery. I decided to come to Sutherdyke and tell you and everyone the truth. I told Mr. Somerby as you danced and waited for Courtney, but when he came I was afraid again. He always terrified me. He would do anything. Once he locked Andrew in a room all day without food. A little baby. Often he beat me. He said that night he would kill me unless I left your house, and I knew he would. In that mood he would do anything. As I went home along the Norhead Road I passed a carriage off the road, hidden in the shelter of a barn. I could only walk slowly, I was so exhausted, and then I heard wheels and hooves behind me and knew it was being driven down on me . . . I felt the horse strike me and was thrown into the ditch. Somehow I scrambled through into the field beyond. He came back and I heard him looking for me for a while, and then he drove away, and I managed to get out to the roadside where Janhoo found me and brought me here . . .'

'How could he have hoped to conceal your marriage?' Dyson said.

'I told you he lived in dreams,' Elspeth said wearily. 'And I had already been silent for four years. He thought he could keep me silent again. Or that I would die — either from despair or from his hand.'

She was silent, turning her head into the pillow, the tears running down her face. I knew she loved him greatly, as I had, that we had been trapped by our first love, our eyes blinded, our ears dumb because we had not wanted to see anything that might tarnish his image.

My aunt rose without a word and went out of the room.

'Poor lady,' said Elspeth.

'Please stay here until you are well,' I said stiffly. 'And do not worry. Be sure that whatever happens neither you nor Andrew will ever want again.'

Dyson followed me out of the room. I was rigid with horror and shock. I would have liked to weep, but could not — he made a gesture towards me, but I shrank back.

'Isabel,' he said, 'don't hate everyone for what Courtney has done to you and this poor woman.'

I looked round the big open landing, down to the great hall and the oriel window. I did not want any of it. I wished I had never seen it. It had brought me nothing but unhappiness and the evil that follows false dreams.

'What shall I do?' I said.

'Soon you will be going to London. It will be a chance to begin your life again.' He smiled. 'What am I saying? You have not started your life yet. You will forget all this, Isabel, and be happy again.'

'No,' I shivered, and said fearfully, 'He will not seek me out?'

'No. I don't think so, not now you know what he is. And I will see that he does not.'

'Thank you.'

I called Janet and we drove over to the Bawtry cottage at Monkstonby, and there I stayed with Bessy until the day came for me to go to London. I could not bear to be at Sutherdyke.

The delay until the Listers were ready to go was unbearable. I found it difficult to talk to people, and stayed indoors, and was grateful for Janet and her mother, their quiet, dour common sense helped, as did their sincere but undemonstrative love.

No one heard from Courtney or saw him — he had apparently left the district. Janet went over to Sutherdyke to get my clothes ready to go to London, and once or twice Dyson rode over to talk business to me — the bank where I could draw money in London, the shops he had arranged for me to have accounts.

They told me his mother was not grieving for what Courtney had done, but only for her missing darling. Her poor face was swollen with tears, her bright chestnut hair, neglected now, was showing grey, and her once elegant appearance neglected. She refused to believe a word of Elspeth's story, she hated me and blamed Elspeth and would speak to no one. As soon as Elspeth was well enough she returned to Ivy Lodge with Andrew, and Dyson saw they were provided for. Immediately after Christmas I left for London.

I was young and healthy, I was rich and pretty and

very much courted — gossip about my early life at the fisherman's cottage went about the drawing-rooms, adding a touch of romance that intrigued people. In London, too, I was still called the Dancer's Daughter. But the social game evaded me — its purpose, stripped of romance, was to find a husband. To find love. I did not want a husband and I was afraid of love.

So the months passed, and I went from gaiety to gaiety, was presented, met a great many people. June came and May Lister had become engaged most successfully to a well-to-do young Yorkshireman from the West Riding, and the Listers were going back home to choose a house for the young couple, buy the trousseau and arrange the wedding. Mrs. Lister was a little worried about me. She confided to her friends, 'Isabel is so beautiful, and such a catch — I quite thought she would be the first to go.' And sometimes she confided to May that she was afraid I was still unhappy over that *terrible* affair, and that it would be a wicked waste if I was left on the shelf because I had given my heart to a rascal.

She was right. I could not give to anyone. I had nothing to give. I looked at every man I met and, however attractive or sincere he appeared to be, I wondered if it were a mask covering an unknown evil or a megalomaniac cruelty.

When the end of June came I could not go back to Sutherdyke. I wrote to Dyson and told him that I would like to travel if the money could be made available and a suitable companion-chaperon found. He came to London to see me, and I was surprised to find how glad I was to see him.

'I did not find a husband, Dyson.'

'I understand it is not for lack of opportunity. You have changed.'

'How?'

'Older, more dignified — more beautiful than ever. Too dignified and too old for someone not yet twenty.'

'You think all this — this plan to travel abroad is a lot of hysterical nonsense?'

'No. I understand. But I think you are running away.'

A small contraction of pain went through me, and I turned aside, trying to sound light and indifferent. 'You used to be cross when I was foolish and impulsive. It seems I can't please you.'

'It does not please me to see you unhappy.'

I told him that I felt travel would improve my languages, that I would like to meet a wider society and see the famous beauty spots of the world. He listened, rubbing his long upper lip with his thumbnail, and smiling a little behind it, and when I had finished said gently, 'It's not only that, is it?'

'No,' I confessed. 'I cannot come back yet, Dyson. Courtney haunts me. Even here in London. Sometimes as I leave a house after a ball I think I see him among the loiterers about the door. Or among the crowds at a race meeting I seem to get a glimpse of his face — that thin burned-out face and those desperate eyes. Then when I stop, he vanishes — I do not know if he is there, watching me, or if I imagine it. If it is like that here, in London, what will it be at Sutherdyke where every room and corner of the garden remind me of him? And where that poor girl he married still lives with his little boy. I want to get right away. Perhaps I can make a new life among new people.'

'For ever?'

'I don't know. A year at least — to find out what I want to do. I shall travel slowly and stay at any place that takes my fancy.'

I sensed him letting me go, relinquishing me, and felt a pain like the tearing of roots, and knew for the first time how much I valued him. How he had been father, guardian and protector to me — I looked at him with new eyes, a woman and not a rebellious child, and saw he was a young man, full of vitality, and not as I had always seen him. Middle-aged, dry-as-dust, over-cautious.

'In December you will be twenty. The following year you will be twenty-one. Then you will have your life and your property in your hands — I will not have the right to advise or restrain you. By then you must know what you want to do.'

'To do with what?'

'With Sutherdyke and everything you own.'

'But you always see to these things. Why should it change? You have always managed everything wonderfully.'

'Isabel, I am not going to work for you all my life. I had a debt to repay to your father and I think I have done it honestly. Did you never think I would leave Sutherdyke and work for myself? I am over thirty. If I am to start it must be soon.'

I had never thought, even when I had most resented him, of life without Dyson or of Courtney replacing him in any way. Not even when I was in love with Courtney and dreamed of the time when we would be married had I really thought of Dyson not being there. I had had a girl's dream of pleasure and love with no tedious responsibilities.

'But I can't manage without you,' I said aghast. 'I don't know how. All those things . . . the money, the investments, the farms, servants . . . papers, accounts . . . what should I do?'

He laughed his abrupt bark of amusement.

'I won't vanish when you turn to find me, Isabel. Be sure when I go I will have found a responsible steward to take my place. Your heart will heal one day, and then you will marry and I hope you will choose someone who will share your responsibilities — for they will be heavy. But in the meanwhile, if you think foreign travel will lay these ghosties of yours, by all means go.'

As usual he arranged my life with flawless efficiency. An old friend of my aunt's, Madame de Crécy, widow of a French diplomat, agreed with pleasure to act as my companion. I took Janet with me, of course. Selfishly perhaps, because the exile in London had been irksome for her and she was longing to get back to the East Riding. But she loved me and understood, and began to pack my luggage for 'foreign parts' with her usual calm acceptance. A courier was engaged, and letters of credit and introduction, and early in September I set out on my goalless pilgrimage.

At first I found it fascinating, and perhaps because I was not quite English, took to the continental life. There was usually a letter from Dyson waiting whenever I arrived at a new city, and my reception had been smoothed in advance.

Dyson was not easily losing his habit of caring for my welfare. I was very glad and began to wait eagerly for his letters. I had teased him, hated him even — rejecting his power over me, resenting his shrewd knowledge of my character. Yet all the time he had grown into my life like a great sturdy oak tree and just the fact that he was there, back at Sutherdyke, watching my interests, caring what happened to me, gave me security and a sense of belonging.

We went to Paris, to Rome, to northern Italy which I loved, and where we stayed for many months. We travelled in Austria and Germany and in my mother's country, Spain. I began to long to return home. I wished Dyson would tell me to come, but I knew he would not. He would help me, but he would no longer make decisions about my life. If I wanted to be free of Courtney I must free myself.

His letters told me of my business investments and interests, the estate, the day-to-day business of Sutherdyke. A little local news. May Lister, now married and living locally, rode my Ladybird sometimes to give her exercise. He had sold the open landau now my aunt rarely went abroad. He worried about her, she was failing, he thought, refusing any knowledge of reality, talking of Courtney as though he were still away in India in the army, and no tragedy had happened. Remembering my wish that Elspeth and little Andrew should be cared for, he had arranged for them to take a small pleasant house on the estate, near the sea. He had difficulty in getting servants to work for her as local girls were frightened of old Janhoo, whom Elspeth would not part from, and who grew increasingly strange.

Sometimes reading his letters I could smell the frost over the fields at Sutherdyke and longed to go straight home, but other things reminded me of the terrible past and made me dread return.

I had been travelling for over a year and the late summer was so hot in Italy that we had come to Nice.

Madame de Crécy was determined to succeed where Mrs. Lister — whom she referred to as 'that provincial lady' — had failed, and find me a husband. With my sophistication and foreign blood she was sure that a titled continental gentleman was what I needed, or if an Englishman someone very cosmopolitan and polished.

This was the last kind of person I admired, and when I attempted to imagine the sort of man I might love I thought of Courtney's ravaged handsomeness and Dyson's stalwart gravity. Emotionally I was still suspended between these brothers and began to wonder if I would never escape. In Nice Madame de Crécy quickly circulated the news of my presence and I was immediately inundated with invitations and callers. Quite suddenly I could stand it no longer, and made my escape. I left her at our hotel in Nice and took rooms in a small *pension* in the mountains at St. Agnes. It had some six rooms and a terrace overhanging the lovely valley. I was alone there, I could wear simple clothes and take long lonely walks. I knew I had to go back home. I could travel no more. I had come to rest, and yet could not make the decision.

One day, too hot to walk at midday, I sat on the terrace above the valley. I had letters to write and a book to read, but I sat idly watching the market carts in the valley. In the dark early hours they had gone to Nice filled with flowers, vegetables and cheeses, and now they were coming back to the mountain villages and farms. The little daily post-cart which came along the valley bringing letters and newspapers began the long pull up the curved mountain road to the town. I put my big straw hat on to go and meet it and collect my letters.

I sat on the wall by the road to read them. The cicadas were filling the summer day with their noisy song. Only one letter — from Madame de Crécy. When was I returning to Nice? It was not *comme il faut* for me to stay alone in that remote place. My friends were asking for me and it was an embarrassment to her. There would be a great concert for charity at the Casino and it was said British royalty would be present, would I not return for this? I pushed the letter into my pocket and opened the first of the parcel of English newspapers that had been sent me. It was dated five days ago and on the first page I read of Courtney's death. Murdered. By Janhoo.

'Mr. Courtney Somerby was found stabbed to death in a room in The Crown at Norhead, East Yorkshire. Mr. Somerby was staying at the inn. The murder was committed by an Indian servant in the employ of his wife. It is said the woman had recently shown an insane hatred of Mr. Somerby. Her body was found later at the foot of the cliffs at Norhead.'

I rose and my knees shook beneath me. Unable to stand I sank down on the low wall again. I was shocked and horrified. I could see the sordid inn, the bare miserable room, smell the heavy sweet scent of the drug which I had once noticed when Courtney took me in his arms. I could see the poor bundle of rags that was Janhoo broken on the fierce rocks at the base of Norhead. I sat blindly looking down the valley, watching a carriage creeping like an insect among the market carts below. I had no grief. No loss, only an overwhelming sense of release. After the storm of desire, the disillusion, the discovery of madness and evil. For the first time since we had parted I could think of him with pity — could see the growing mania of self-deception which had made him what he was, and then, for the first time, wondered if I had ever loved him. Knew that I had never really known him — that the boy I had loved so passionately had not existed — at least not for many years.

I opened the locket on the chain about my neck, and took out the little coil of vine tendril which Courtney had given me with such charm and tenderness. My engagement ring. It was brown and brittle, and as I took it out broke into bits — I crumbled them into dust, and tossed them over the wall into the breeze that blew down the valley. He was dead. It was finished. I was free.

The carriage which I had been watching with indifferent eyes turned from the valley road up the steep hill to the village which hung like an eyrie on the mountain side. Once again I experienced that white flash of premonition. I could hear the water in the fountain, the thrumming voices of the drinking pigeons, the cicadas' shrill song, but I was caught again in the white light of knowing. I knew Dyson was in that carriage and I knew it was what I wanted more than anything on earth.

The children gathered as it drew up and the old woman who sold lace hobbled forward. Occasionally tourists made the journey from Nice to see the picturesque walled village and to lunch at the one good restaurant.

It pulled up the slope behind the sweating horse and came to a stop in the small cobbled *place* by the church. I saw Dyson get out. He carried his hat and his jacket over his arm. His plain North-country clothes were unsuitable in this climate. I thought 'He's come to take me home,' and was filled with an extraordinary happiness. I rose from my seat on the wall and went across to him. He saw the newspaper in my hand.

'You know?'

'Yes. Just now. You came to tell me?'

'I did not want you to read it like this. When I had your letter to say you had come up here to the mountains I thought you might not see an English paper and if I came at once I might get here before you knew.'

'You have travelled all this way to save me pain? So I should not be alone when I read of his death?'

'Yes.'

I put out my hand and touched him, laid it on his broad chest. His shirt was damp from the hot drive in the enclosed carriage. I could feel the great vitality of him beating beneath my fingers. He changed colour, and caught my hand in his — it was a strange declaration, more sweetly sensual than all the passionate kisses I had known.

'You are not grieving — you are no longer haunted! You are free of him at last?'

'I was long before this happened. But I have just re-alised it. Tell me what happened.'

He drew my hand through his arm and we went up the

narrow street of donkey steps to the pension and sat on the terrace under the shade of the vine trellis.

'Apparently you really were haunted, Isabel. For a long while — all the time you were in London he followed you, watching you from a distance, not daring to speak or approach you.'

I shivered, but I was glad that I had not imagined that face that appeared among the crowds.

'Lately he was ill ... he went down into the depths, with drink and drugs. He borrowed on his income, and could not meet the debt. He came to The Crown about a month ago, and the landlord took him in. He had always gone there since he was a young boy, to escape from his mother's reproaches, perhaps from me. If we forbade anything he would run there and stay, thinking we would give in, and my mother always did, of course. He learned to drink there and to gamble, and finally he came back there, penniless and sick. I went to see him. I saw he was comfortable, had medical care, but I forbade him to get in touch with our mother, or with his wife. It was wrong of me, perhaps, but he had already caused them such distress. My mother might not stand the shock — and Elspeth has begun to find a little peace and hope.'

'You must not blame yourself about him. You always have — I know that now.' He looked up questioningly. 'Now I don't blame you any more. I understand how you have blamed yourself.'

'We were so different,' he said helplessly. 'I could never understand him. But then I had not his looks or charm, so I had not the temptation of vanity or dreams. He hated me, and I tried not to hate him. But there is only five years between us — he and my mother treated me as an old man, to shoulder all their responsibilities. All his follies. Sometimes the burden was intolerable.'

'And then you took on the further burden of me.'

He shook his head and I saw tears in his eyes.

'Nay, Isabel. You were a torment to me sometimes, but never a burden.'

'Go on — tell me what happened.'

'He promised to leave them in peace, but he could not keep his promise. He wrote to Elspeth. He had heard she was living in comfort. He asked her for money — to get him out of debt again. He said if she did not help he would come and live with them. He had a right to bring up his own child. Elspeth was so distressed and frightened that it roused Janhoo to a fury of revenge. She must have remembered the night of your ball, when she had found her mistress unconscious and half dead after he had tried to kill her. She went to The Crown that night, found out his room, and killed him. It was a bad night of high gale and rain storm, and next morning she was found on the shore below the high cliffs. Whether she took her life or lost her way, we cannot know. Elspeth was broken-hearted — Janhoo was a burden to her, but devoted and loyal.'

He talked of Elspeth now, familiarly, as one often seen and well known.'

'You are fond of Elspeth?' I said.

'Very. And of the boy. She is one person who will never escape from Courtney. Janhoo was right. She would have gone to him and she would have helped him in spite of her terror. She is a marked woman. Whatever he did she will love him until the day she dies.'

'And your mother?'

I have told her of his death, but did not tell her how. She did not believe me. Courtney, she says, is still in India, having a brilliant army career, popular and successful, for ever absent — for ever young. She reads his early letters from India, and tells me old news as though it happened yesterday. It is tragic, but I think she is happier for it. She has one consolation — the little boy Andrew. He is not like

Courtney in any way, but there is a little trick of lordliness that reminds her of him. She pretends she does not know who he is — or who his mother is. But she visits him every day.'

'Now I can forgive him — and he was not entirely to blame. It was I who suggested that we should run away. I think until then he was resisting the temptation of loving me. Now I know I did what I did from childish defiance. To show you — you were not my master. Not really for love.'

We were sitting close together, my hands still in his.

'No one will ever be your master, Isabel. I know that.' He looked at me, and asked, 'And now are you ready to come home?'

'Dyson — once long ago you told me that young things, puppies and birds, remain devoted to the first human being who is kind to them and feeds them. When I came to Sutherdyke as a child I was out of my depth and insecure. I was rather frightened of you. I was humiliated by your mother. But Courtney was sweet to me and I never stopped to think why and just gave him all my love in gratitude. Now I know that I owe everything to you — what I am, what I have. And if at first what you did was from duty, later it was from love — you do love me, don't you, Dyson?'

'So very much.' I moved forward on to my knees beside him, so that my head was against his shoulder and I was sheltered and encircled by his big body. I heard his breath catch as he said, 'Why are you telling me this now?'

'I want you to understand all about me — why I was so unreasonable and sometimes so unkind,' I went on determinedly. I *wanted* him to understand. 'I want to be with you at Sutherdyke. I know you love me — this I know as certainly as I knew that Courtney could never harm me and I knew that it was you driving up the hill just now. It must be being half-gypsy — I see things white and clear. But even if you love me, you may not want me — you may really want to get away from me and Sutherdyke and all that it has meant. But I will go back there, anyway. I'll try to do what you have tried to teach me. To shoulder my responsibilities, to care for people who depend upon me and run my affairs honestly, but oh, Dyson,' — my voice was tinged with despair, 'I hope you do want me, for it will be a long and lonely way without you . . .'

He stood up, bent and put his hands beneath my arms and lifted me like a doll until my eyes were level with his. The tears were running down both our faces — the big man and me. I put my arms round his neck.

'I'm trying to tell you how much I love you,' I said. 'I'm wanting you to ask me to marry you and take me home. I've discovered what I want. That's what I want — you and me, together for always. If I have that, nothing else would matter — nothing else at all.'

So he kissed me, and said all the things I longed to hear him say, and I knew then that I had come home.

THE DEVIL'S INNOCENTS

JOSEPHINE EDGAR

Excluded from the dances and games of her friends by a
slight lameness, Barbara Crossdyke had never over-
come her natural shyness, or ventured from the sheltering wing of her father's love. But in the space of one
stormy night her tranquil existence was shattered, when
a handsome young Spaniard, Ramon Ramirez, was
carried wounded and unconscious into her home – and
into her heart.

Deeply in love Barbara agreed to follow Ramon to
Barcelona to meet his family. But the welcome awaiting
her in the home of these severe aristocratic people was
not what she expected. Should she have listened to her
faithful servant's prophesies of danger and death? Had
she come to Spain as a bride, or as a prisoner?

CORONET BOOKS

HISTORICAL ROMANCE FROM CORONET

JOSEPHINE EDGAR

- ☐ 20775 2 The Devil's Innocents   35p
- ☐ 18784 0 My Sister Sophie   35p
- ☐ 18783 2 The Dark Tower   35p
- ☐ 18782 4 Time of Dreaming   35p

MARY ANN GIBBS

- ☐ 18985 1 The Romantic Frenchman   35p
- ☐ 18984 3 Horatia   35p
- ☐ 19349 2 The Penniless Heiress   35p
- ☐ 20508 3 The Amateur Governess   35p
- ☐ 20514 8 A Parcel of Land   60p

All these books are available at your local bookshop or newsagent, or can be ordered direct from the publisher. Just tick the titles you want and fill in the form below.

Prices and availability subject to change without notice.

CORONET BOOKS, P.O. Box 11, Falmouth, Cornwall.

Please send cheque or postal order, and allow the following for postage and packing:

U.K. — One book 18p plus 8p per copy for each additional book ordered, up to a maximum of 66p.

B.F.P.O. and EIRE — 18p for the first book plus 8p per copy for the next 6 books, thereafter 3p per book.

OTHER OVERSEAS CUSTOMERS — 20p for the first book and 10p per copy for each additional book.

Name ....

Address ....

....